GUNSMITH GROUPIE . . .
OR HIRED GUN?

The desk clerk beckoned Clint closer.

"Yes?" Clint said.

"I thought you should know, sir," the man said, "that there was a man here asking about you . . ."

"Would you know him again if you saw him?"

"Oh, yes sir. In fact, I see him now . . . the lobby sofa to the left . . . against the wall. He is seated there . . . "

Clint turned and started for the stairs, stealing a look at the man on the sofa. He didn't know him . . . The man was fair-haired, good-looking, and well dressed. He did not look like a Westerner.

Suddenly, Clint had a bad feeling . . .

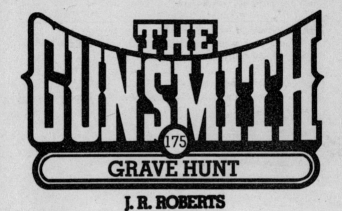

THE GUNSMITH

175

GRAVE HUNT

J. R. ROBERTS

JOVE BOOKS, NEW YORK

GRAVE HUNT

A Jove Book / published by arrangement with
the author

PRINTING HISTORY
Jove edition / July 1996

The Putnam Berkley World Wide Web site address is
http://www.berkley.com

ISBN: 0-515-11896-6

A JOVE BOOK®
Jove Books are published by The Berkley Publishing Group,
200 Madison Avenue, New York, New York 10016.
JOVE and the "J" design are trademarks
belonging to Jove Publications, Inc.

PRINTED IN THE UNITED STATES OF AMERICA

10 9 8 7 6 5 4 3 2 1

ONE

Clint Adams looked across the poker table at a familiar face, but it was a face he had no better luck reading on this day than he had the first time he saw it.

The face belonged to Luke Short, and this hand had come down to Clint and Short, as many had.

Also at the table were Bat Masterson and two other players: Ben Thompson and a man named Brett Garner.

The game had started several days earlier with three tables of eight players each, and had come down to these five players.

The game was five-card stud. In front of Clint, faceup, were a two, three, and five of spades. In front of Luke Short were three queens. There was one card left to come to each player. The others had folded after three cards.

"Your bet, Mr. Short," the dealer said.

There had been six rotating dealers when the contest began, and now two of them were dealing an hour on and an hour off.

Since all of the money from all the entrants was on this table, the betting had gone up drastically. It was a winner-take-all tournament with $24,000 as the prize.

"Two hundred," Short said.

Clint had an ace of spades in the hole. He needed a four of spades or he wouldn't even be able to beat Short's three queens. If Short filled in, or made four queens, it would be overkill. If, however, Clint made his four, his straight flush would take the hand no matter what Short did.

It was times like this you took the plunge.

"Call two hundred," Clint said.

There was no point in raising. Short knew Clint couldn't possibly have anything until the fifth card was dealt. There would be no bluffing him.

"Fifth card comin' out," the dealer said.

Luke Short got his card first and it was an ace of hearts. Clint's card was dealt to him, and the four of spades skidded across the table to join the other spades. He had his straight flush.

Short had to figure Clint for a flush, or a straight flush. A simple flush would beat three queens, but not a full house, and not four queens.

"Five hundred," Short said.

Most of the money on the table was sitting in front of him. Clint and Bat had most of the rest. The other two players were almost out of the game.

, "Call five hundred," Clint said, "and raise a thousand."

"You son of a bitch," Short said to his friend. "You made your straight flush."

"I could be bluffing, Luke," Clint said.

Short shook his head.

"You'd know you couldn't bluff me out," Short said. "Not when I'm sitting here with four queens—but you don't care that I have four queens, do you, Clint?"

Clint said nothing.

"No," Short said, "you'd want to see them."

"And you'd want to see my card, wouldn't you, Luke?" Clint asked.

"I have to see your card, Clint," Short said, "because if I don't call, you'd never tell me, would you?"

Clint didn't answer.

"I didn't think so."

Short tossed the thousand-dollar raise into the pot.

"Let's see the ace."

Clint flipped over the ace.

"Damn," Short said, and flipped the fourth queen. "I don't believe I could lose a hand of five-card stud with four queens."

Clint raked in his chips and said, "Ninety-nine times out of a hundred, you wouldn't have."

Short nodded as the dealer collected the cards.

Clint now had most of the money in front of him, and it looked like he was about to start a run toward the entire $24,000 pot.

On the next hand Ben Thompson busted out of the game, and left quietly. That hand was taken by Brett Garner, though, and suddenly the youngest man at the table got hot and started to win.

Losing with four queens seemed to have taken it out of Luke Short, and he couldn't buy a hand from that point forward. He was the next player out of the game, leaving Clint, Bat, and Garner.

"Time for a break," the dealer said.

The $24,000 looked to be portioned out evenly among the three players at that point.

"Care for a drink?" Bat asked Clint.

"Why not?"

The game was being held in a private room at the Denver House hotel, and Clint and Bat went down to the bar for a drink. There they encountered both Luke Short and Ben Thompson.

"Looks like the youngster's got you boys on the run," Short said.

"At least we're on the run," Bat said.

Thompson glared at Bat. It was well known that the two men did not like each other. Clint, on the other hand, counted both men as friends—as well as Luke Short. It was Bat, however, who Clint knew the longest and best. He had met Bat and Wyatt Earp at the same time, but over the years he had crossed paths with Bat more than with Earp.

If Clint Adams had a best friend, it was Bat Masterson.

"That young man is a fine poker player," Short said.

"He ain't that much younger than me," Bat complained.

"He ain't seen thirty yet, Bat," Short said. "You'll never see it again."

"That still ain't much," Bat griped.

"Ben, are you going to stick around to see who wins?" Clint asked.

"I'm gonna stick around until this drink is gone," Thompson said, "and then I'm on my way."

"How can you leave without knowing who the winner is?" Bat asked.

"That's one of the differences between you and me, Bat," Thompson said. "If I ain't the winner, I don't care who is."

With that he downed the last of his drink and set the empty glass on the bar.

"See you fellas around," he said, and left.

"That's a cold fella," Bat said.

"You just don't like him," Short replied.

Bat shrugged and said, "He's cold, anyway."

"Ho, what have we here?" Luke Short said.

Clint and Bat also noticed the woman who was approaching them. She was well dressed and attractive. Her dark hair was piled above her head, revealing a long, graceful neck. Her skin was alabaster, as if it had never been kissed by the sun.

"I've got fifty dollars that says she wants to talk to me," Bat said.

"You're on," Clint said.

"No bet," Luke Short said. "I know she's gonna want to talk to one of you Romeos before she'll want to talk to me."

"Okay then," Bat said, under his breath so only they could hear him, "let's see."

TWO

As the woman came closer, Bat Masterson brought himself up to his full height, which was still a couple of inches shorter than Clint. Luke Short, the shortest of the three, didn't even bother to straighten up. He kept his elbow on the bar.

"Gentlemen," the woman said. Up close they saw that her eyes were the most arresting shade of violet.

"Can we help you, ma'am?" Bat asked.

"You can if one of you is Clint Adams."

Bat's face fell and Clint smiled.

"I'm Clint Adams," he said. "How can I help you?"

"Is there someplace we can talk?" she asked.

Clint checked the time. Their twenty-minute break was almost up.

"Actually, I'm pretty busy at the moment—"

"Playing poker, I know," she said. "I heard about the tournament. Are you winning?"

"I'm ahead, yes," he said.

"A pity," she said.

"What's that?"

She smiled, embarrassed by her remark.

"I'm sorry, it's not that I wish you ill luck, but if you were losing I could perhaps buy your time."

"My time is not for sale, miss."

"Mine is," Bat said, but she ignored him.

"Please," she said, "it won't take a minute."

"These gentlemen are my friends, miss," Clint said. "This is Bat Masterson, and that slouched over fella is Luke Short."

"I am pleased to meet you both," she said. "Of course, I know who you are."

That puffed Bat's deflated ego up a notch.

"You can say what you have to say in front of them."

"I only want to ask for your help," she said. "I understand you often help those in need."

"Oh, you've got that right, ma'am," Bat said, slapping Clint on the back. "He is always ready to help someone in need."

Clint ignored Bat and studied the young woman in front of him. She looked to be in her late twenties, but might have been thirty or more. Her dress had not come cheap, and she did not look as if she was in need of anything—and he said so.

"No," she said, "not in that kind of need. I have money. What I need is help."

"With what?"

"Finding my father."

"Why would you need help doing that?"

"I'm from the East," she said, "and he left there almost twenty years ago."

"To go where?"

"Here," she said, spreading her pretty arms. Clint could see that her arms were well toned, which indicated she was no stranger to hard work. "To the West."

"And you don't know where he went?"

"It's sort of . . . complicated."

Clint checked the time again.

"We've got to go, Clint," Bat said.

"I know."

"Oh, please," she said, putting her hand on Clint's arm. "If I could just talk to you when you're through with your game?"

"I don't see why not," Clint said, "if you want to wait."

"I don't mind," she said. "How long will it be?"

"A few hours . . ."

"I can wait—"

". . . or a few days. It all depends."

She fell silent, then said softly, "I'll wait . . . if you don't mind."

"I don't mind, Miss . . . ?"

"Benton," she said, "Jodi Benton."

"Miss Benton," he said. "Where will you be?"

"I will be here," she said. "I'm staying in the hotel."

"All right."

"There's one more thing you should know about my father."

"What's that?"

"He's dead."

Both Bat and Clint stopped in their tracks and turned to look at her.

"What I need help finding," she added, "is his grave."

THREE

The woman looking for her dead father's grave intrigued Clint, but he knew he wasn't going to win the tournament if he gave her too much thought. As it turned out, young Brett Garner stayed hot and did away with Bat Masterson first, and then came down to a final hand with Clint.

The result of that final hand showed Clint how Luke Short had felt when Clint beat his four queens. Clint had four tens and bet confidently against what Garner was showing, which was three jacks and a king. Not having played Garner except for this competition—and then only for this one day—Clint was unable to read whether the man was bluffing that fourth jack or not. He could have held on to the last few hundred dollars of his money and tried to build it up, but when was he going to see a hand like this again—especially since he'd already had a straight flush? What were the odds of another hand like those two, when there had been so many bad hands in between them?

He called Garner's last raise and showed his four tens. When the young man turned over his fourth jack, the dealer said, "Mr. Garner wins."

Clint stood up and extended his hand across the table.

"Well played," he said.

Garner, who had remained stoic throughout, now smiled and said, "I can't believe I won, not against you and Bat Masterson and Luke Short, not to mention Ben Thompson—"

"Enjoy it," Clint said, giving the younger man's hand a last shake, "because it won't be long before you'll be looking at us again across a poker table."

"I'm looking forward to it," Garner said.

"So am I," Clint said. He shook hands with the dealer, and left the room.

It had been five hours since he'd seen Jodi Benton, and that made it two in the morning. He found Luke and Bat sitting downstairs in the bar, which was almost empty. Clint got a beer from the bartender and joined them.

"You lost," said Bat, who had busted out of the game two hours earlier.

"Four jacks to four tens the last hand," Clint said, sitting down.

"Now you know how I felt, you bastard," Short said.

"I can't believe we let that . . . beginner beat us,"

Bat said, shaking his head. "We're gettin' old."

"He got all the cards in the end, Bat, that's all," Clint said.

"Oh, good," Bat said, smiling, "then we're not gettin' old."

"I am," Short said, "I don't know about you."

"Where are you headed after this, Luke?" Bat asked.

Short thought a moment, then said, "California, I guess. Maybe San Francisco."

Bat made a face.

"I just came from San Francisco."

Short smiled and said, "I know. I'm not lookin' forward to sitting at a poker table with you again, so I'm goin' the other way."

Bat smiled and said, "We got to lick our wounds, huh? Well, in that case I think I'll go to Chicago. I heard tell of a game there." He looked at Clint. "What are you going to do about that girl looking for her father's grave?"

"I don't know," Clint said.

"You got something to do?" Short asked.

"No."

"Someplace to go?" Bat asked.

"No."

Both men shrugged.

"So help her," Bat said. "She looks like she could be very grateful."

"And she did say she had money," Short said.

"Sometimes you sound so damned mercenary, Luke," Bat said.

"And you are always tryin' to get under some young woman's skirts."

"What's wrong with that?"

"What's wrong with wantin' money?"

"Nothin'."

"Okay," Short relented, "so there's nothin' wrong with you, either."

"I'm going to bed," Clint said.

"What's the hurry?" Bat asked.

Clint looked around.

"They want to close."

Bat frowned.

"I hate goin' to bed alone."

"Don't you have a wife somewhere?" Luke asked.

"Yeah," Bat said, "somewhere. I guess I'll go to bed, too."

"Sounds good to me," Short said, standing to join the other two. "Where do you suppose that kid is headed next?"

"I don't know," Bat said, "and I don't care. We'll catch up to him soon enough."

All three of them were staying in the hotel, their rooms free as part of being in the game. They walked to the second floor, and while Bat and Short went to the left, Clint went to the right, all the way to the end of the hall. By the time he got to his door, Bat and Short were in their rooms.

Clint fitted his key into the lock and opened the door. He smelled her before he saw her lying in his bed, and he was so quiet entering that he didn't wake her.

He turned the wall lamp up just enough to see her face, expecting Gloria Cummings, a woman he had slept with twice while in town. It was not Gloria, though, because she was blond and the head on his pillow had black hair.

He moved closer to the bed and was surprised when he recognized Jodi Benton.

FOUR

Clint stared down at her for a few moments, stunned by her beauty in repose. As if she could tell he was looking at her, she suddenly opened her eyes and stared back at him. Their violet color was even more stunning against the whiteness of the sheets. Or were they lavender?

"Hello," he said.

"Hello."

"What are you doing here?"

"I needed a place to sleep."

"I thought you said you had a room here at the hotel," he said.

"I thought I would," she said, "but when I went to the desk they said they had no more rooms."

"How did you get them to let you into my room?" he asked.

She smiled.

"I told the clerk I was going to wait here to congratulate you when you won. Did you win?"

"No, I didn't."

"Oh."

Abruptly she tossed the sheet back, revealing herself to be naked.

"Then what shall I congratulate you for?"

He was momentarily stunned into silence. He hadn't expected to find her in his bed, and he certainly hadn't expected to find her there naked.

Her body was very pale, except for the black bush between her legs, and the dark brown nipples of her full, rounded breasts. She was full-bodied, with the belly and thighs of a woman, the way he liked them.

"Well?" she asked.

"What do you think this is going to get you, Miss Benton?" he asked.

"Call me Jodi."

Her name was the only thing that seemed girlish about her.

"I hope to get a place to sleep," she said, "and maybe somebody to sleep with."

"Are you trying to use your body to get me to help you?"

She frowned and propped herself up on one elbow. The movement did interesting things to her breasts.

"Now what would that make me?" she asked.

"You tell me."

She reached out and put her hand on him. She

could feel his hardness through his pants. She got to her knees and started to undo his gun belt.

"Have you thought that maybe I just want someone to be with tonight?" she asked. "I've come a long way to do something I dread. All I need tonight is a little comforting."

"And that's all?"

His gun belt dropped to the floor and she undid his trousers belt.

"That's all."

He grabbed her wrist as she undid his pants.

"This doesn't buy you anything. Understand?"

"I understand."

She pulled her wrist free, put her arms around his neck, and kissed him. Her lips were full and soft, but her kiss was firm. This lady meant business, and now that he'd tasted her kiss, so did he.

He pushed her away from him so that she fell back on the bed in a seated position. Her eyes looked like they were on fire, and her nostrils were flaring as she breathed—and her breaths came harder as she watched him undress.

Clint recognized the look when he saw it. This was a woman who loved sex, and was single-minded when indulging herself. In this case, he was perfectly willing to be as single-minded as she was.

He put one knee on the bed, and she reached out and took his erection in her hands. He closed his eyes as her fingertips inflamed him further, then pulled her hands from him and pushed her back until she was lying down on the bed.

He held her wrists above her head and kissed her, plunging his tongue into her mouth. She moaned as he clasped her wrists in one hand and began to explore her body with the other. He slid his hand down between her breasts, over her belly, and between her legs. He probed into her bushy pubic hair until he found her, already wet. He slipped his middle finger into her and she jerked, as if struck by lightning.

He released her wrists, and she wrapped her arms around him as he kissed her neck, her shoulders, and then her breasts, still sliding his finger in and out of her, up and down, stroking her, stoking her fire to a fever pitch.

She moaned and writhed beneath him until she finally bit his shoulder hard enough to make him cry out. In return he bit her nipple hard enough—he thought—to take revenge, but when she laughed and said, "Harder," he knew he was in for a rough night.

The first time he entered her he was on top of her. She gasped and wrapped her legs around him, but after just a few moments of that she surprised him with her strength by turning them over so that she was on top.

She straddled him, looking down at him with those amazing violet eyes. Her black hair was a mess, and she looked like a wild woman as she rode him hard, sliding up and down him, her hands on his chest for leverage. He took her breasts in his hands and sucked the nipples hard while she continued to bounce on him. Suddenly, he felt her body tense and she threw her head back and cried out. . . .

Moments later he chose the position, getting behind her while she was on her hands and knees. His erection was still rock hard and pulsing, because he hadn't allowed himself to finish yet. He slid one hand between her legs to stroke her, but she pushed her butt back against him and said, "Now, now!"

He obliged her by getting up on his knees behind her and poking his penis through her thighs and into her.

"Oooh, God," she cried out, and started to move forward and back, slamming into him hard each time she met his thrust. The bed began to rock in place, so violent were their motions. At one point he reached for her and got a handful of hair. He knew he must be hurting either her hair or her neck, but she didn't complain once. They continued to slam against each other over and over until he couldn't control himself any longer. He exploded into her and she hollered and buried her face in the pillow to muffle her cries. . . .

FIVE

In the morning she woke him with her mouth, avidly taking him inside even before he was fully hard. He could only reach for her head and cup it while she rode him up and down with her mouth, moaning as she did so, getting to her knees in her excitement as he neared his climax. He tried to prolong it, but she was too good and too anxious for him and finally he could hold back no longer. . . .

"Is your game over?" she asked later, lying in the crook of his arm.

"Yes."

"Where do you go from here?"

He put his other arm—the right one—behind his head and stared at the ceiling.

"I don't know."

He waited for her to ask him for help again, but she didn't.

"Who won? Mr. Masterson?"

"No."

"Mr. Short?"

"No."

"Then who?"

"Are you really interested?"

"Yes."

"A man named Brett Garner."

"I never heard of him."

"Neither did I, until this week."

"A stranger beat you, and Mr. Masterson and Mr. Short?" she asked, surprised.

"That's right."

"That's surprising."

"It surprised us, too."

"Wouldn't you like to play him again?"

"We will," he said, "sometime."

There were a few moments of silence, and when she spoke again he thought she was finally going to ask.

"I'm hungry," she said instead.

"So am I."

"Can we go downstairs and have breakfast?"

"Sure," he said, "if we're done here."

She smiled and kissed his left nipple, flicking it gently with her tongue.

"We're finished here," she said, "for now."

He watched as she got up and began to dress. She stood in front of the mirror and said, "Oh, God, I've got to do something with my hair."

"All right, all right," he said suddenly, "tell me about your father."

She turned to face him. The bodice of her dress was open, revealing most of her breasts. With her hands she was holding her hair above her head.

"I said I wouldn't ask, remember?" she said. "This night didn't buy me anything?"

"I know what I said, Jodi," he said. "I'm the one who's asking, all right?"

"As long as we're clear on that."

"We're clear."

"Good," she said, turning back to the mirror, examining herself critically. "Let me do something with my hair, and we'll go down to breakfast and talk."

"I'll get dressed," he said, getting up from the bed.

He shook his head as he dressed. He knew that he'd done this to himself by allowing her to stay in his room—and his bed—last night. She knew it, too, and she had played him perfectly by not even mentioning her father when morning came.

He was going to have to watch this one, he thought. She was devious.

SIX

They dressed and went down to the dining room for breakfast. For all of the fussing she did about her hair, she looked perfect to him. No one would have guessed that he'd had his hands wrapped in that hair for half the night.

Jodi Benton was, by far, the most energetic bed partner he'd ever had. There was nothing she wouldn't do, or try, and she seemed impervious to pain. The harder he bit her, or drove himself into her, the more excited she seemed to get, the more she seemed to want. Women who liked pain did not appeal to Clint, and he had known a few, but Jodi was different. She didn't like inflicting pain—he'd been with a woman once who wasn't satisfied unless she'd marked him—and she didn't *insist* on or need pain to be satisfied, but a little pain certainly didn't do anything to cool her passion.

Sitting across from her he couldn't see the woman he'd been in bed with. This one was cool and calm, very collected, very ladylike. He'd never known a woman who underwent such a change when she was naked.

They ordered breakfast and he was impressed that her appetite matched his. There were a lot of facets to this lady, and he found himself looking forward to studying them all.

Once they had coffee in front of them, Jodi told her story.

"I was born in Philadelphia twenty-six years ago," she said. "Twenty years ago my father left my mother and me and came west. That is, he started west, intending to come here, to Denver. He was a newspaperman, and he felt that there was need in the West for men like him."

"Go west, young man?" Clint said.

"Something like that, yes," she said.

"How did he travel?"

"I'm not sure," she said. "My mother died soon after he left, a sudden death that left me orphaned. It was not until I turned eighteen that I actively started trying to find my father."

"And you've been looking all this time?"

She nodded.

"I've sent telegrams all over the West, trying to find anyone who knew him. Early this year I finally got some word on him."

"That he was dead?"

She looked down.

"Yes." She looked up again. "I heard from a man

who said he traveled with my father on a wagon train through Nebraska."

"When?"

"The man was old, and he was vague about everything except for one thing."

"That your father died."

"Yes," she said, "and was buried somewhere along the route."

"But he didn't know where."

"No."

"Where is this man now?"

"He's dead, too," she said. "I found that out by coming here. He died last month, shortly after I received his telegram."

Their breakfast came at that moment and they suspended the conversation until it was served and the waiter was gone.

"Now," she continued, "I'm stuck here and I don't know where to turn."

"How did you hear about me?"

She shrugged.

"I've talked to so many people. I know someone mentioned your name and that there was a big poker game here this week. I just came here on the chance you'd still be here . . . and that you'd be receptive to helping me."

"Well, I was receptive to something," he said.

"That was not a ploy to get you to help me," she said. "I swear."

Clint didn't know whether he believed her or not, but he decided to let it pass for that moment. They both started to eat their steak and eggs.

"Nebraska," he said. "That's all you know?"

"Well, I know they started from Council Bluffs,

Iowa, and that he died somewhere in Nebraska."

He thought a moment.

"We'd have to find someone who remembered the route they were going to take, and then we'd have to retrace that route."

"I knew you'd know what to do."

"It won't be easy, Jodi. It would involve lots of riding in the sun, and your skin doesn't look like it would take it very well."

She touched her face.

"I'll get used to it."

He didn't say anything.

"Clint, if you could just give me some idea of what to do and how to do it, that's all I'd ask. I mean, if you don't have the time—"

"You couldn't do this alone."

"I'll hire someone."

Clint could just imagine the kind of man she'd end up with.

"That wouldn't work."

"Why not?"

"You wouldn't know who to hire," he said. "Look how you found me."

"I could find someone else the same way."

"You got lucky with me, Jodi."

She smiled and said, "Don't I know it?"

"I don't mean that," he said. "Another man would take advantage of you."

She smiled again.

"I don't mean that way," he said again. "Be serious. You told me you have money. If you say that to the wrong man you'll end up robbed, or worse."

Her look sobered.

"I see what you mean."

"You can't just walk up to some men at a bar and ask for help. You'll get the wrong kind."

"What you're saying, then," she said, "is that I need you."

"Well, yes—I mean, no—well, someone like me—"

"Are there many men like you?"

He paused and stared at her.

"There are a few."

"Probably fewer than you think," she said.

"Have you thought about just going home?" he asked her.

"To where? Philadelphia? That hasn't been my home for some time. I don't have a home, Clint. I want to find my father, bury him properly, and then I can start thinking about finding a home for myself."

Clint stared across the table at her for several minutes, until she started to fidget.

"Clint?"

"All right, Jodi," he said. "I don't have any definite plans for the next few . . . weeks. I'll help you."

"Oh!" she said, and for a moment he thought she was going to throw herself at him.

"Hold on, now," he said, holding up his hand. "There are some conditions."

"Anything."

"You've got to prove to me you can ride."

"I can."

"And you'll have to do what I tell you without hesitation."

"I will."

"You're not used to this kind of traveling."

"I know."

He stared at her and then said, "Without question. Is that understood?"

"Understood," she said.

"Why do I think you'll be more trouble than you're worth?"

She smiled and said, "I don't think you think that at all."

"I think you're strong-willed and used to getting your own way."

"Maybe."

"That won't work with me."

She smiled and said, "I know."

"I think I'm getting in over my head."

"When do we leave?"

"A few days," he said. "I want time to outfit you, and us for the trip, and to see what kind of horsewoman you are."

"They have horses in Philadelphia, you know."

"I know," he said. "Finish your breakfast and we'll shop some today."

"I like shopping," she said. "I'm good at that."

"Where is your luggage, by the way?"

"The hotel is holding it for me."

"I'll have it moved to my room . . . that is, if it's all right with you."

"It's fine with me."

Clint set about to finish his breakfast, feeling as if he had been totally outfoxed. He wondered idly if Jodi Benton had ever played poker.

SEVEN

They spent the day outfitting Jodi for the trip. First they got her luggage moved to Clint's room so he could inspect her clothing. She had nothing that she could use on the trail. She got upset when Clint said she was going to have to leave it all behind, but he reminded her that she had agreed to do what he said without question, and she grudgingly gave in.

They went down to the lobby, intending to go shopping but ran into Bat Masterson as he was checking out of the hotel.

"Miss Benton," Bat greeted, giving Clint a look. "When will you be leaving, Clint?"

"Not for a few days."

Bat smiled at Jodi.

"I see you convinced him to help you."

"Clint has agreed to help me because he knows I'd be helpless without him."

"I see." Bat gave his friend another look.

"Why don't you wait for me by the door, Jodi."

"All right."

"Good-bye, Miss Benton."

"Mr. Masterson, it was a pleasure to meet you."

"The pleasure was all mine."

As she walked away out of earshot, Bat said to Clint, "Or is it all yours?"

"She needs help, Bat."

"I know," Bat said, "that's what she said last night, when you refused. What changed?"

"I just decided to listen to her problem."

"And she made a convincing case for helping her, huh?" Bat asked.

"You have a dirty mind."

"Hey," Bat said, "if a woman who looked like that asked for my help, I'd give it. You're not doing anything I wouldn't do . . . are you?"

Clint put out his hand and Bat took it and shook it warmly.

"It was good to see you, Bat. I hope I'll see you again soon."

"You will, my friend," Bat said. "Maybe back here. I like Denver a lot."

"Where's Luke?"

"Checked out earlier."

"Sorry I didn't get a chance to say good-bye."

"He told me to say good-bye for him. We'll all cross paths again."

"Bet on it," Clint said.

As he turned away Bat asked, "Do you want any

help with Miss Benton . . . I mean, with her problem?"

"I know what you mean," Clint said, "and no, I don't need any help."

"Pity."

"Bat," Clint said, shaking his head, and went to join Jodi.

"What was that about?" she asked.

"He was offering his help."

"Do we need it?"

"If we do," Clint said, "it'll still be there. Come on, let's get you some clothes. I hope you were serious about having money."

"I have enough to shop with."

"I hope so."

EIGHT

First they shopped for the proper trail clothes for her.

"Not very stylish," she complained when they began.

"You don't need stylish, you need practical."

"I don't think I've ever shopped practical before."

"Don't worry," he said, "I'll help you."

None of the clothing they bought would have been her choice, but they were what she needed for the trail.

They stopped for lunch at a small café Clint knew, and piled Jodi's packages beneath the table.

"What's next?" she asked.

"A hat," he said, "and then a horse."

"I like hats."

"Maybe we'll find one you like that's also useful."

"And practical?"

"Yes."

They did find something that satisfied both of them after lunch. When it was time to look for a horse, they took all the packages back to the hotel first and had a bellboy take them to the room.

"I need for you to be completely truthful with me now, Jodi."

"About what?"

"About your riding ability."

"I'm a very good rider."

"Do we need to find you a gentle horse?" he asked. "Or a genteel horse?"

"I don't think so," she said. "I'm really a very good rider, Clint."

"Have you ridden with a western saddle?"

"Yes," she said, "I've ridden with all sorts of saddles."

"I think I'm going to have to see you ride for myself to decide."

"Suit yourself."

They went to the hotel livery where Clint rented a horse for Jodi, a bay mare that was neither tame nor wild, but somewhere in the middle. He then saddled Duke while she watched.

"My God," she said when she saw the big black gelding, "this is a horse? He's huge."

"Duke *is* my idea of a horse," Clint said, pulling the cinch tight on his saddle.

"Duke?"

"That's his name."

She reached for Duke's head and Clint said, "Careful, he doesn't like people much."

He watched in surprise as Duke suffered Jodi's touch, and then seemed to lean into it as she stroked his nose.

"He seems to like me well enough," she said.

"Yes," Clint said, "he does, doesn't he?"

She looked at Clint, still stroking the gelding's nose, and asked, "Does this win me some points?"

"It wins you a lot of points," he said, "with Duke. I still want to see you ride."

"Skeptic."

Once Duke was saddled, they both mounted up. Clint watched with approval as Jodi swung herself gracefully into the saddle. He watched, too, how she handled the reins as they rode their horses out of the livery, behind the hotel, where there was an open field that led to some woods.

"Just ride ahead of me," Clint said.

"And do what?"

"Cut left, cut right, wheel her around. I want to see how you handle a horse."

Jodi did as she was told and by the time she was done Clint was satisfied.

"Well?" she asked.

"You'll do."

"Now you've got to catch me," she said. She wheeled the mare around and kicked her in the ribs. Clint gave her a head start and when she was almost to the woods he nudged Duke into a gallop.

NINE

He took his time closing the gap so he could watch how she handled a horse at a full run. By the time he caught her—easily, once he let Duke run—he was convinced that her riding was not going to be a problem.

He drew abreast of her and reached over to grab her horse.

"So?" she asked.

"Don't ever use a horse like that unless you have to," he said.

"It's fun," she said. Her face was flushed with excitement.

"We're not going to be doing any riding for fun," Clint said. "We'll probably be putting in a lot of miles, and we'll have to conserve our animals. The time may come when we'll have to run them, and I want them to be in condition for that. Understand?"

"Yes," she said contritely, "I understand."

"How do you like that mare?"

"I like her fine."

"Okay then," he said, "let's go on back and see if we can buy her."

"Does she have a name?" she asked as they started back.

"I doubt it," Clint said. "They don't usually name horses they're renting out."

"Good," she said, "then I'll call her . . . Misty."

"Why?"

Jodi shrugged.

"I like the name."

"That's as good a reason as any, I guess."

"Why did you call your horse Duke?"

"Because he looks like a Duke," Clint said. "He's always looked like . . . royalty."

"Then why not Prince, or King?"

Clint made a face.

"Those sound like dog names."

She looked surprised.

"You're right, they do."

They rode in silence for a while, and then she said, "We've gotten a lot done today, Clint. Do you think we could leave tomorrow?"

"I don't think so," he said. "Rein in, here."

They stopped and he said, "Get down."

She dismounted.

"Ground your reins."

She dropped them to the ground.

"Why don't you ground yours?"

"Duke's not going anywhere."

"Why did we stop?"

"Can you shoot?"

"A gun?"

"Yes, a gun."

"I can shoot a rifle."

Clint didn't have a rifle with him. His was in his room. He took his revolver from his holster.

"Have you ever fired a revolver?"

"Yes," she said, "but I'm not very good with one."

"Show me."

She took the gun from him.

"What shall I shoot at?"

"That branch." The branch was about twenty feet away and about as thick as a man's leg.

She aimed the gun, closed one eye, fired and missed the branch, and the tree.

"Okay," he said, "this time keep both eyes open and just point the gun, don't aim it."

"Point?"

"Like it was your finger."

She did as he said, pulled the trigger, and missed the branch—but this time she hit the tree trunk.

"That was better," he said. "This time squeeze the trigger, don't pull it or jerk it. Okay?"

"I'll try."

"Don't try," he said, "do it."

She nodded.

"Can I hold the gun with both hands?"

"Sure, why not," he said, "but remember, point it, don't aim it."

She nodded again, then pointed the gun, took a deep breath, squeezed the trigger . . . and hit the branch.

"I hit it!"

"Now put the next three shots right in the center of the tree trunk."

"All right."

"Think of it as a man's torso."

"What?"

"The tree trunk is a man," Clint said. "He's coming at you to do you harm. Shoot him."

"But—"

"Shoot him now!" he snapped.

Startled, she raised the gun and fired quickly, missing with all three shots.

Clint walked over to her and took the gun away. He ejected the empties and inserted fresh cartridges into the gun before holstering it.

"We might run into trouble along the way, Jodi," he said. "It's possible you might have to fire very quickly at a man, without thinking. If that happens, you're going to have to be able to hit him. If you don't, he'll kill you."

"You yelled—"

"He's going to do a lot worse than yell at you," Clint said.

She took a deep breath, rubbed her sweaty palms on her thighs, and said, "Let me try it again."

"No," Clint said. "That's enough for today. Tomorrow we'll buy you a gun that will fit your hand, and we'll come back here and try again. All right?"

"A-all right."

"Let's mount up and get back. We have to see if we can buy Misty for you."

TEN

The man in the livery used the excuse that he was not supposed to be selling horses to drive a hard bargain, but he finally relented and for a hundred dollars Misty was Jodi's.

"That's enough shopping for one day," Clint said as they left the livery and started back to the hotel.

"I need a bath."

"I do, too," Clint said, "and afterward we can have some dinner."

"Good," she said, "I'm famished. Riding usually makes me hungry."

They entered the hotel and Clint said, "There's a bathtub in the room. I'll talk to the desk clerk about having it filled. Why don't you wait in the room."

"All right."

They split up. She went to the stairs and he went to the front desk. Neither of them noticed that they were being watched by a man sitting on one of the lobby sofas.

"Can I help you, Mr. Adams?" the desk clerk asked.

"I need some hot water brought to my room."

"Right away, sir."

Clint turned to go upstairs but stopped when someone called his name.

"Clint?"

He turned and saw Jefferson Baines approaching him. Jeff Baines had been the host of the poker tournament. A wealthy man in his early forties who loved playing, he had been one of the first to bust out of the game, but he enjoyed watching good poker players at work.

Baines had arranged for suites or rooms at the hotel for all of the players, and Clint wasn't sure if the man had a piece of the hotel or not.

"I thought you'd gone," Baines said. "I was sorry I hadn't had a chance to say good-bye."

Clint shook hands with the man and said, "I'm afraid I'll be around a few more days, Jeff."

"Wonderful. Perhaps we can have dinner."

"Maybe another night. I have a dinner engagement tonight."

"Fine, fine," Baines said, releasing Clint's hand. "Quite a surprise ending to the tournament, wouldn't you say?"

"Yes, I would say," Clint said. "Where did you find that young man, anyway?"

"He came recommended," Baines said. "He was very good, wasn't he?"

"He was good," Clint said, "but whether or not he is very good remains to be seen. He got amazingly hot there at the end."

"Yes, he certainly did. Well, perhaps I can put you boys together again sometime?"

"I'm sure you could."

"In fact," Baines said, "Mr. Garner isn't leaving Denver yet, either. I'll bet I could arrange a private game. Just for us? I know some players who would be interested."

"That's a possibility, Jeff," Clint said thoughtfully. "That's a definite possibility."

"It would give you a chance to win your entry fee back."

"Yes, it sure would. Get back to me on that, will you, Jeff?"

Baines smiled broadly and said, "I'll get right on it."

Baines walked away and Clint was about to do the same when he heard his name again. This time it was the desk clerk.

"Yes?" Clint said.

The clerk beckoned him closer.

"I thought you should know, sir," the man said, "that there was a man here asking about you."

"Was there?" Clint said. "What did he want to know?"

"Just if you were registered here."

"And?"

"I'm afraid the fellow I replaced told him that you were."

"Then this was an exchange you overheard?"

"Yes, sir."

"Did you see the man?"

"Yes, sir."

"Would you know him again if you saw him?"

"Oh, yes sir. In fact, I see him now."

"You do?"

"Yes, sir."

"Where?"

"Behind you."

"Where exactly?"

"The lobby sofa to the left when you turn, sir," the clerk said. "Against the wall. He is seated there."

"Is he alone?"

"At the moment, yes."

"What do you mean, at the moment?"

"When he was here earlier," the clerk explained, "he had another man with him."

"Did he also approach the desk?"

"No, sir, he stayed back, but they were together," the man said. "I could tell."

"Was there anyone else with them?"

"No, sir."

Clint took out five dollars and tried to give it to the man.

"That's not necessary, sir," the clerk said. "I'm just doing a service for a guest."

"A much appreciated service, too. What's your name?"

"William, sir."

"Thank you, William."

"I'm glad I could be of service, sir."

Clint turned and started for the stairs, stealing a look at the man on the sofa. Clint didn't know him. The man appeared to be in his thirties and, judging from the length of his legs and torso, fairly tall. He was fair-haired, good-looking, and well dressed. He did not look like a Westerner.

Suddenly, Clint had a bad feeling.

The man on the sofa—Dennis Pelter—watched
Clint Adams go up the stairs, and kept his eyes on
him until he was out of sight. He stood up, then, and
left the hotel. He turned right and started down the
street to a less expensive hotel where he and his
partners were staying.

Adams had spotted him. He was sure of that. He'd
tried to be nonchalant about it, but it was part of
Pelter's job to follow people, so he knew when he'd
been spotted. It had been a momentary flicker of the
man's eyes, very brief, but enough.

It was important that he let his partners know this
as soon as possible.

ELEVEN

When Clint got to the room, Jodi was already in the tub of hot water. The Denver House had great service for their guests, and this was just another example. While he'd been talking to the clerk and Jeff Baines, a bellboy had come up and filled the tub with hot water.

"Did you flirt with him?" Clint asked.

"Of course," Jodi said from behind the screen that hid the tub from sight. "And if you come around here I'll flirt with you, too."

Clint had undressed as quietly as he could and came walking around the screen naked, his penis semierect.

"Is the tub big enough for both of us?" he asked.

She smiled and reached out, stroking him with one wet hand.

"I'll *make* room."

She drew him closer, still stroking him with her wet hand, and he stepped into the tub. She released him so he could sit across from her. He placed his legs outside of hers, then reached for her and drew her to him. His erection poked her and she laughed, reaching for it with both hands. The head of his penis broke the surface of the water. She encircled him with one hand and stroked the head with the other.

He grew impatient. He reached down into the water, slid his hands beneath her buttocks, lifted her up, and then impaled her on his rigid cock. She leaned back and he kissed the wet slopes of her shiny breasts and suckled her nipples.

She groaned and put her head down on his shoulder as they started to move together, creating waves in the tub. Their movements were gentle enough to keep the water from overflowing, but insistent enough to cause waves to build up within them, until finally they both crested at the same time. . . .

They made love in the tub, careful not to flood the room. Afterward they made love again, on the bed this time, getting the sheets wet in the process—and not only from the bathwater.

After that they dressed and went down to the hotel dining room for a late dinner.

"God," she said, when they reached the lobby, "I was famished before our bath. Now I could eat a horse."

"Well don't," Clint said, "we just bought it for you."

"Oh, I would never eat Misty," she said, as a waiter

led them to a table. "I could never eat a horse I had ridden."

"Happens all the time out here," Clint said.

"It does? That's horrible."

"Not if you're hungry enough," Clint said. "I know men who have eaten horses, mules, even dogs."

"Dogs?" She made a face. "Please tell me we're not going to have to eat a dog while we're looking for my father's grave."

"I don't think that will happen."

"Have you ever eaten dog meat?"

"Yes."

"When?"

"Times when I've been with Indians," he said. "When you're with the Indians you eat what they cook, and dog is a delicacy to them."

"Oh, yuck!"

She said this just as the waiter came over to take their order.

"Ma'am," he said, "I assure you our food will never deserve that kind of talk."

"Oh, I'm sorry," she said, waving her hands, "we were talking about something else."

Jodi let Clint order for both of them, since he had eaten in the hotel before. He ordered steaks and vegetables, and a pot of coffee. As the waiter moved out of his line of sight, he saw Brett Garner sitting across the room, eating alone. If he hadn't been with Jodi he would have asked the younger man to join him. Eating a meal with someone can help you get to know them better; and knowing Garner better would have been useful the next time they played poker. Of course, by the same token Garner would have gotten to know him better, as well.

Over coffee she said, "You really enjoy coffee, don't you?"

"Good coffee," he said. "Black and strong."

"I make good coffee."

"You'll get your chance to prove it," he said.

"I can do all the cooking on the trail."

"That won't be necessary," he said. "We can share the cooking."

"Cooking is women's work, isn't it?"

"Not to any man who's ever ridden on the trail," Clint said. "Also, when you go on a trail drive the cook is usually a man. No, there's little out here that can't be shared by a man and a woman, in the way of work."

"Sewing?"

He shook his head.

"I do my own sewing, and I've even darned a sock or two."

"Washing?"

"When I'm traveling alone I've got to do my own washing. There are men who won't do it, but they're not fellas you'd want to be around for any length of time."

"I think you must be an amazing man—I mean, in a lot of ways."

He shook his head, unsure of what to say.

"And modest," she added. "I understand you have a reputation with a gun."

"Lots of people have a reputation with a gun."

"You mean like Bat Masterson?"

"Bat and I both have reputations that are a little . . . exaggerated."

"What about with cards?"

Clint laughed.

"Now there Bat's reputation may even be a little understated."

"Is he a better player than you?"

"Oh, yes," Clint said readily, "and Luke Short is probably better than both of us."

"And yet you all lost to this newcomer?"

Clint grimaced.

"Don't remind me."

"Well," she said, "everybody gets lucky once, right?"

"I'll try to keep that in mind."

TWELVE

They continued to eat dinner, and Jodi noticed Clint glancing over at Garner.

"He doesn't seem aware that you're here," she said.

Clint smiled.

"He knows."

"Any chance of another game between you two?"

"Funny you should ask," Clint said. "The man who arranged the week-long game has asked if I'd like to play in a private game before I leave Denver."

"And would he—I'm sorry, what's his name?"

"Brett Garner."

"Would Garner be willing to play?"

"I imagine so," Clint said. "After all, he is twenty-three thousand dollars ahead."

Jodi started to look around the dining room.

"Are there any other players in the room?"

"No," he said. "I think they've all left town."

"Then who would play?"

"There's always somebody willing to play poker."

"Especially with the Gunsmith?"

"I don't really like being called that."

Jodi looked immediately contrite.

"I'm sorry."

"No, I'm sorry," he said. "I didn't mean—it's just not a name I think of myself by, that's all. I have a question for you."

"I'll answer it, if I can."

"Do you know a tall, fair-haired man . . ." he asked, and went on to describe the man he'd seen in the lobby of the hotel.

She thought a moment, then said, "No, I don't think so. Why?"

"He was in the lobby today, asking about me," Clint said, "and he looks like an Easterner."

"So you thought I'd know him?" she asked. "There are a lot of cities in the East, Clint."

"I just wondered if there was something you're not telling me."

"What? That someone else wants to find my father's grave? I'm afraid I'm the only one with that particular mission in life."

"Okay," he said, "I'm sorry."

"Is it unusual for you to be watched, followed, or asked about?"

"Unfortunately, no. I guess I'll have to look elsewhere for my answer."

"I'm sorry I can't help."

He still wasn't sure she couldn't help, but he decided not to press the point now.

"Are you worried about this man?"

"Well, if he's just another reputation hunter I don't want to put you in danger."

"Maybe we should leave tomorrow, then."

"No," Clint said, "we still have some work to do with you."

"The next day, then?"

"Certainly within the next few days."

"I'm sorry I'm impatient," she said. "It's just that—well, now that I have somebody to help me I'm starting to hold out real hope that I'll find my father—his grave, I mean."

"You can't go off half-cocked, Jodi," Clint said. "We'll leave when I'm sure we're ready to leave."

She sat back in her chair and said, "I'll leave myself in your hands."

"Good," he said, smiling, "because I like you there."

"And I like being there."

They stared at each other across the table for a few moments until the waiter came.

"May I clear, sir?"

"Oh, yeah, sure."

"More coffee?"

He looked at Jodi, who shook her head.

"No," Clint said, "we don't need any more coffee, thanks."

THIRTEEN

Down the street three men sat in a much smaller room than Clint Adams had at the Denver House hotel. One of them was Dennis Pelter, the man who had been watching Clint Adams in the lobby of his hotel.

"Are you sure he saw you?" Joe Sullivan asked.

"It's my business to know, Joe," Pelter said. "He saw me."

"Well," Sullivan said, "what's it matter? He doesn't know you." He looked at the third man in the room. "He doesn't know any of us."

"That doesn't matter," the third man said. "Now he knows somebody is interested in him."

"So what do we do?" Pelter asked.

"Nothing, for now," the third man said. "He's got a rep. Lots of people watch him. Lots of people are

51

after him. He's always careful. We'll just have to be more careful than he is."

"So we're gonna go ahead with this?" Pelter asked.

"Yes."

"Why don't we just take care of him now?" Sullivan asked.

"What would that accomplish?" the third man asked.

"It would get him out of our way."

"But would it get us any closer to what we're looking for? No. If we leave him alive, though, and follow him and the girl, they just might."

"I don't see—"

"Why don't you boys go out for a walk?" the man said, cutting him off. "I need some time to myself."

"I just wanna—"

"Let's go, Joe," Pelter said, tossing the man his jacket.

Sullivan wanted to argue with someone, but he didn't know who, so he just got up and followed Dennis Pelter out of the room.

The third man's name was Mace. At least, that's what he had Sullivan and Pelter calling him. They didn't need to know his real name. They were just hired muscle.

Mace wondered if he'd made a mistake bringing hired men from the East with him, and not hiring them when he got to the West. It certainly wouldn't hurt to have someone with them who knew his way around the West.

They still had time to hire someone. He didn't think Clint Adams and Jodi Benton would leave Denver for a couple of days yet. They had to get to know one another, and they still needed some supplies.

That's what he'd do, then. He'd use today and to-morrow to find somebody else to take along with them, someone who was familiar with the territory.

With Clint Adams in the picture, they were going to need all the help they could get.

FOURTEEN

They went back to the room and exhausted each other—at least, Jodi became exhausted. After energetic lovemaking she fell into a deep sleep. Oddly, Clint, though pleasantly physically fatigued, was not sleepy. He slipped from the bed without waking her, dressed, and went down to the hotel bar.

The bar was all leather, crystal, and mahogany, nothing like the Western saloons he was used to. Actually, the differences between the two was why he liked to come to the bigger cities, and when he grew tired of them it was nice to go back to the simplicity of the small Western towns.

He walked to the bar and ordered a beer. The bartender knew him from his stay. But the man was an oddity for a bartender. He didn't talk much. He simply nodded and set the beer in front of Clint.

Clint picked up the beer and turned to lean against the bar. Seated at a corner table, dealing solitaire, was Brett Garner. To the young man's left was a beer mug that was almost empty.

"Give me another beer," Clint said to the bartender.

Carrying two beers, he walked across the half-filled room to the table Garner was seated at.

"Looks like you could use another beer," he said.

The man looked up and recognized him immediately.

"Hello, Mr. Adams. Yes, I could use another one. Thanks."

Clint set the mug down next to the almost empty one.

"Have a seat," Garner invited.

"Thanks."

Clint moved around and sat with his right side to the wall, so he could see the entire room.

"Do you want this chair?" Garner asked. He was sitting with his back to the wall.

"This one will do," Clint said. "You played a hell of a game this week."

"I played well," Garner said. "Toward the end I got unbelievably lucky."

During the game Garner hadn't talked much. Clint was trying to place the man's accent now, and he thought he had it.

"You're from New Orleans."

Garner looked surprised.

"That's right. I thought I'd lost the accent."

"On purpose?"

Garner shrugged.

"I just haven't been home in a very long time."

"Is that where you learned to play poker?"

Garner shrugged again, placing a red queen on a black king.

"I picked it up along the way."

"Like solitaire," Clint said. "Black three on red four. You missed it."

"Thanks," Garner said, moving the card. "No, I'm a little better at poker than I am at solitaire."

"A lot better, I'd say. I understand Jeff Baines is trying to set up a private game. Did he invite you to play?"

"He did."

"And?"

"He invited you?"

"Yes."

Garner grimaced.

"What's that mean?"

Garner looked at him.

"To be frank, I'm not sure I want to push my luck with you."

"Ever?"

Now Garner smiled.

"No, I mean this week. I'm sure we'll play again, sometime."

"Is this all you do?" Clint asked. "Play cards?"

"I'm afraid I'm ill-suited for anything else. You're rather good at it for someone who doesn't do it full-time."

"Thanks."

"Why don't you do it full-time?"

Clint thought a moment, then said, "I'm afraid if I had to depend on it to make a living I wouldn't enjoy it as much."

"And what do you do to make a living now?"

"This and that," Clint answered. "I've got some money put away."

"I'm trying to do that," Garner said.

"This week helped, I'm sure."

Garner smiled sheepishly, as if embarrassed that he'd won.

"Yes, it did."

"Be nice to have a chance to get some money back."

"Are you saying you'd like to play again?"

Clint shrugged.

"I still have a couple of days in Denver."

"So you're saying that you're going to play in that private game?"

Clint finished his beer and stood up.

"I might."

"Well then," Garner said, "maybe I will, too . . . just for fun."

"Just for fun," Clint repeated.

"Thanks for the beer," Garner said.

"Sure," Clint said, "anytime."

Garner started dealing out a new hand of solitaire as Clint left the table. He watched Clint until he was gone, and then put the cards down. He picked up the fresh beer, drained half of it, and set it down. He picked up the cards again and started playing, wondering what Clint Adams would say if he knew what "Brett Garner" really did for a living.

FIFTEEN

Clint paused in the lobby to check it out. He didn't see the man who'd been watching him, and nobody seemed to be watching him now. He saw the same desk clerk in place and went over to talk to him.

"Sir?"

"Anyone asking for me since I saw you last, William?" Clint asked.

"No, sir."

"Have you seen either of the men who were looking for me?"

"No, sir."

"All right."

"If I see them, sir, would you like me to try and find you?"

"Yes, I would," Clint said, "or leave a message for me."

"I'm happy to help, sir."

"Thanks. Oh, one more thing."

"Sir?"

"Do you know Jefferson Baines?"

"Yes, sir, I know Mr. Baines very well."

"Can you give him a message for me?"

"Certainly, sir."

"Tell him I'll be available to play."

"Yes, sir, I'll tell him."

Clint admired the desk clerk because the man asked very few questions.

"I appreciate it."

"We're here to serve our guests, sir."

"Well, I think you go a little beyond your job, William, and I thank you."

The clerk nodded, looking embarrassed at the praise.

Clint decided not to embarrass the man anymore and went back to his room. Jodi was still in bed, sleeping soundly. The room smelled of their sexual exertions and Clint found himself responding to the scent. He didn't want to wake her, though—not yet, anyway—so he walked to the window and looked out. The street in front of the hotel was dark and there wasn't much he could see. Someone could have been standing across the street watching the hotel and he wouldn't know it.

He toyed with the idea of going out for a walk, but if someone was watching for him he'd be painting a target on his back by walking around the streets in the dark. He'd painted a target on his back many times in the past to draw someone out, but those times he usually had some idea of who it was. In this case he'd be operating blind, and he wasn't willing to do that.

"What is it?" Jodi asked.

He turned to look at her. She had propped herself up on one elbow and was looking at him sleepily. Her long black hair fanned out wildly, and she used one hand to try and move it away from her face. She looked primal and he felt his body responding to the way she looked, and the way the room smelled.

"It's nothing," he said. "I was just looking out the window."

She rubbed her eyes and said, "I woke up and you were gone. Where did you go?"

"Just downstairs for a while."

"Is everything all right?"

He walked to the bed and sat down. He put his hand on her thigh and could feel her warmth through the sheet.

"Everything is fine."

"You were looking for those men, weren't you?"

"What men?"

"The ones who were asking about you."

"Not exactly," he said. "I had a conversation with Garner."

"About the poker game?"

"Yes."

He was rubbing her thigh through the sheet, and now he pulled the sheet away from her so that there was nothing between his flesh and hers. He ran his hand over her thigh and hip, then up to her breasts.

He teased her nipples with his palm and she closed her eyes.

"Get undressed," she said, lying on her back. "Come back to bed."

She didn't have to ask him twice.

SIXTEEN

Clint woke first in the morning. He'd gone to bed early for him, and so woke even before first light. He was amazed, after they'd made love several more times during the night, that he felt so awake. Jodi was fast asleep next to him.

He lay there next to her until the sun started to filter through the window. He sat up, swinging his feet to the floor, and she didn't stir. He knew she'd probably miss him again when she awoke, like last night, but he couldn't lie in the bed anymore, and he didn't want to wake her.

He got up and got dressed quickly and quietly. He strapped on his gun, which he'd been keeping on this trip. There were times when he was in a bigger city— where it was more "civilized"—when he sometimes left his Colt in his room in favor of a little New Line Colt he could hide in his belt. For some reason, though, he'd been wearing his regular Colt, and now he had more reason than ever to keep it on. Somebody was asking questions about him, and that was always reason enough.

Fully dressed he left the room, Jodi still fast asleep in bed.

When he got down to the lobby, William was still on duty behind the desk. The man looked at him and shook his head, as if he could read minds. Clint nodded his thanks. It was comforting to know that no one had been around looking for him during the night.

Clint hesitated there in the lobby. He was torn between having breakfast in the hotel and going out for breakfast. Going out would still make him a possible target, but at least it was light and he'd have a chance to spot potential danger.

His decision was made for him when his name was called. He turned to see Jefferson Baines approaching.

"I'm glad to see you up so early—or are you still up?" Baines asked.

"No, I'm up early."

"Good, good. Have you had breakfast?"

"No."

"Then have it on me. Come on, we can talk about the game."

"The game?"

"The private game."

"Oh, yes, that game."

"What game did you think I meant?" Baines asked, slapping him on the back.

"There are all kinds of games, Jeff," Clint said. "All kinds."

Baines walked Clint right into the dining room to a table without the benefit of a host or a waiter. Further indication that he might be a man of importance in the Denver House hotel, like a part owner.

A waiter came over and took their order, acknowledging Clint's request for coffee as soon as possible, and then adhering to it.

Over coffee Baines said, "I saw Brett Garner last night, in the bar. I thought you might be there, too."

"I was," Clint said. "I saw Garner, bought him a beer, and then went to bed."

"Did you talk about the game?"

"We discussed the possibility of it."

"It's a reality," Baines said excitedly. "He agreed when I saw him. All we need is you."

"For when?"

"Tonight?"

"And who else is playing?"

"Well, me," Baines said, "and three other players."

"You don't have the other players yet?"

"Well, not the exact players, no," Baines said, "but I have a list."

"What kind of list?"

"A list of men who are interested in playing against, uh, talented poker players."

"And who are the men on this list?"

Baines smiled.

"Rich men, powerful men, influential men," he

said, "politicians, businessmen—even the chief of police."

"Let's leave him out of this, okay?"

"Done. Then you agree to play?"

"Sure," Clint said, "why not."

"Good, good."

"But you've got to do something for me."

"Like what?"

"I get the impression you can make things happen around here."

"I'm not without influence," the man said modestly.

"I want a new room."

"That's easy."

"But I don't want anyone to know," Clint said. "In fact, I want it to look like I've checked out."

"I can do that," Baines said. "Can I ask why?"

"Somebody was here asking about me yesterday."

"Yes?" Baines said warily. "And what were they told?"

"That I was registered here. I don't want that kind of information given out."

Baines frowned.

"Who gave it out? I'll have his job."

"I don't want anyone's job, Jeff," Clint said. "Just give me what I want."

"Okay, you've got it. When?"

"I've got a lady staying in my room with me," Clint said. "Let's wait until she's up and around."

"All right."

"I trust William, out front," Clint said. "Can I give him the word?"

"William's a good man," Baines said. "Yes, by all

means, just let William know when you want it done, and it'll be done."

"Fine," Clint said. "Thanks."

Their breakfast came at that point, steak and eggs for Clint, and just some buttered biscuits for Baines.

"I'll finish this up and make the arrangements for your room change, and for the game tonight."

"Will the game be in the same room?"

"Yes. Is nine all right?"

"Fine."

"This will be good, seeing you and Garner going at it again."

"This is the only night, Jeff," Clint said. "I'll be leaving tomorrow morning."

"I'll be sorry to see you go," Baines said. "But you'll be back, right?"

"Sometime."

Baines nodded in satisfaction.

SEVENTEEN

Baines finished his breakfast first and excused himself from the dining room. That left Clint alone to ponder the immediate future. "Checking out" of his room might throw whoever was looking for him off the scent, but not for long. He was moving up his timetable for their departure for that reason. He'd have to continue Jodi's education on the trail. Today could have been for buying her a gun, and maybe a little training with it, but he would probably keep her inside, just to be on the safe side.

Of course, there was still the possibility that she knew more than she was saying. Clint had been lied to before. Sometimes he just expected it of people. Other times he thought he wasn't giving people enough of a break.

He was looking forward to finding out which was which with Jodi Benton—and he wasn't putting any money on either way.

He finished his breakfast and was told by the waiter that the bill had been taken care of by Mr. Baines.

He left the dining room and went back up to the room to tell Jodi about the change of plans.

"You're really worried about this man who was looking for you, aren't you?" she asked, packing her bags.

"I'm being careful," he said.

"Because of me?"

"To keep us both safe."

She put her hands on her hips.

"If it wasn't for me I don't think you'd be doing this."

"If it wasn't for you I probably would have left Denver today," he said, "but that's neither here nor there now. I've agreed to help you, and I'm not going to go back on my word now. I am, however, going to do what I can to keep you from being hurt by someone who's coming after me."

"So we'll be leaving tomorrow?"

"Yes," he said, "and staying in another room tonight."

"Will you be playing poker tonight?"

"I'm supposed to," he said, "but if you don't feel safe—"

"Nonsense," she said. "You go ahead and play. Who knows when you'll get another chance?"

"I won't be playing too late," he said. "I want to get an early start in the morning."

"What about supplies?"

"We'll have to arrange for them today."

"And a gun for me?"

"I have one you can use," he said, thinking of the New Line, "until we can stop somewhere and buy you one."

She paused in her packing to look at him.

"Clint, I can't tell you how much I appreciate everything you're going through."

"Tell me after we've found your father's grave site," he said. "You keep packing. I'm going downstairs to tell the desk clerk that we're ready to move."

"All right."

She went back to packing until Clint left the room. When he was gone she stopped and went to the window to look out. She hoped that whoever was asking about Clint was someone who was after him and not her.

Clint went downstairs and told William that they were ready to move.

"Very well, sir," William said. "I'll have two trustworthy bellboys go up and do the moving."

"I'll go up and wait for them."

"Yes, sir."

"Thanks, William."

William gave him what was by now a patented blank look and said, "Just doing my job, sir."

"I know, William," Clint said, "I know."

Clint went back upstairs to wait with Jodi for the bellboys.

EIGHTEEN

They were moved to a room on the same floor, but at the opposite end of the building. Their window overlooked an alley in the back. It was the same as the suite they had moved from, identical in size and layout.

Clint tipped the two bellboys and hoped, as they left, that they were as trustworthy as William said they were.

"Will we be all right here?" Jodi asked.

"We'll be fine."

"What about that gun you promised me?" she asked. "I mean, just in case I should need it while we're still in Denver?"

"That's a good idea," he said.

He went to his bag and took out the Colt New Line.

"It's so small," she said as he handed it to her.

"It'll do the job," he said. "Just remember what I told you. Aim for the torso." He placed his hand flat against his chest. "Squeeze the trigger, don't jerk it, and point it, don't aim it. Can you remember that?"

"I think so."

"One more thing."

"What's that?"

"If someone is coming at you," he said, "just keep pulling the trigger until the gun is empty."

"Shouldn't I just fire once or twice and save some shots?"

He shook his head.

"If you fire once you might never get another shot," Clint said. "Fire as many times as you can, and get as many hits as you can. You want him to go down and stay down."

"A-all right."

"Will you be able to do that?"

"If my life is in danger," she said, "yes."

"Good."

"What should we do now?"

"Well, you might not like this," he said, "but I think you should stay in this room until we leave tomorrow."

"You're right," she said, "I don't like it. What will you do?"

"I'm going to talk to someone and see if I can't get our supplies delivered right to the livery."

"That way neither one of us has to go outside to buy them."

"Right," he said. "Remember, we're supposed to have checked out."

"Right."

"Can I count on you to stay inside?"

"Will you come back and spend some time with me?"

"Yes."

"All right," she said. "As long as you don't leave me alone. I'll go stir-crazy."

"You can count on me to keep you company."

She went to him and put her arms around his neck.

"Quality time, Clint Adams," she said, "I want quality time."

He smiled and said, "That's the best kind, ma'am."

NINETEEN

Clint went downstairs and had another conversation with William at the desk. In the end he gave William a list of supplies. The desk clerk promised that the supplies would be waiting for them with their horses the next morning.

That done Clint was at a loss as to what to do with the day. He probably should have forgotten about the poker game so they could have left that morning, but he'd already given his word to Jeff Baines, and he didn't want to break it.

He couldn't leave the hotel. He didn't want to be seen now that he'd "checked out." What was there to do in the hotel, though? He knew what he and Jodi would do if he went back to the room, but as good as that was, they couldn't do it all day.

Could they?

He decided to go back to the room.

They managed to while away the morning and part of the afternoon before they decided to go downstairs and get some lunch.

"Is it safe to go down?" she asked.

"The man who was looking for me is not a guest," Clint said, "and unless he's in the lobby I think we're safe in the hotel."

"What if he is in the lobby?"

"This time I'll make sure I have a talk with him. Are you hungry?"

"Very," she said. "Satisfying you is very hungry work, Mr. Adams."

"That's just what I was thinking about you, Miss Benton."

"It is miss, isn't it?" he asked ten minutes later in the dining room.

"What?"

"I never asked you if you were married or not."

"No, you never did . . ."

Clint had come downstairs first, to check out the lobby, and then called for Jodi to come down.

When they went to the dining room the man who showed them to their table had said, "Mr. Baines has said that you are to have his private table anytime you come down, Mr. Adams."

"Well, tell Mr. Baines I appreciate it."

Baines's table was in the back, and Clint noticed that it was more separated from the rest of the tables than any other.

"Would you like a screen?" the man asked as he seated them.

"A screen?"

"A partition," the man said, "to give you some privacy."

"Uh, no, this is fine," Clint said.

"Why didn't you want the screen?" Jodi asked, after they were seated.

"I want to be able to see the rest of the room."

Now he was waiting for her to answer his question about being married.

"Are you?"

"No," she said, and then added, "not anymore."

"So you were?"

"Yes, at one time."

"How long ago?"

"We were . . . divorced recently."

"Can I ask why?"

"Too many differences of opinion," she said. "Roger and I just didn't see eye-to-eye on anything."

"Roger."

She nodded.

"Roger Mason."

"What did he do for a living?"

"A lot of things," she said, "not all of them legal."

"Oh," Clint said, "a businessman."

"He kept a lot of lawyers in business."

"Is that where your money came from?" Clint asked. "Him?"

She nodded.

"I had a good lawyer, too," she said. "After it was all over I decided to use my divorce settlement to try and find my father. That was something Roger was never willing to help me do."

"Why not?"

"He thought the whole thing was silly," she said, "that I'd want to find a man I hadn't seen in years."

They paused to give the waiter their lunch order. This time they each handled their own.

"Why don't you?" she asked after the waiter had gone.

"Why don't I what?"

"Think I'm being silly."

"I just don't think it's silly to want to find your father."

"Do you know where yours is?" she asked.

"No."

"Wouldn't you like to know?"

"He's dead."

"I thought you said you didn't know where he was?"

"I meant," he said, looking up, then down, "I don't know where he went."

She laughed at his joke—if it was a joke—and then asked, "What about your mother?"

"Boy," he said, "I really am hungry."

"I get it," she said. "You get to ask questions about me, but I don't get to ask any about you."

"Ask away," Clint said, "there are just some I'll answer and some I won't."

"How will I know which is which?"

"I'll give you a hint," he said, "by not answering."

TWENTY

As it turned out, Clint answered about half of Jodi's questions, as most of her questions were personal.

"This isn't fair, you know," she said after an hour of grilling. They had finished their dinner, their dessert, and were now having an after-dinner pot of coffee—at least, Clint was.

"I've been asking you questions for an hour and I still know very little about you."

"That's the way I prefer it."

"Oh, a man of mystery, are you?"

He hesitated, then took a deep breath and plunged in.

"I'll tell you something you haven't asked."

"Oh, good," she said, resting her chin in her hands. "I'm all ears."

"A lot has been written about me," he said. "Most of it is inaccurate, some of it is lies, and very little of it is true."

"So if I were to read everything that's been written about you I'd still know very little, wouldn't I?"

"Yes."

She leaned back in her chair.

"How does someone get to know you, Clint?" she asked. "I mean, really know you?"

"By not asking questions," he said. "By spending time with me, watching me, listening to me, by letting me answer by my actions questions that aren't asked."

She stared at him for a moment, then shook her head, as if to clear it.

"You're a complex man, Clint Adams," she said. "Maybe too complex for me."

"Me?" he asked. "Too complex for an intelligent woman like you?"

They laughed, and he looked around for the waiter to get their check.

In another part of the hotel two men sat opposite each other in easy chairs.

"Where did you get my name?" one man asked.

"I asked around," the man called Mace answered.

"You were obviously asking in the right places," the other man said. "How did you know to do that?"

"I believe there is a network for this kind of thing," Mace said.

"All over the country?"

Mace shook his head.

"A worldwide network."

The other man stared at him.

"I don't deal on a worldwide scale," he said, "not usually, anyway."

"That's all right," Mace said. "The job I want done is right here in the United States. In fact, it will start right here in Denver."

"And why do you need my particular talents for this job?"

"Because my associates and I are from the East," Mace said. "We know very little of the West. Also, we'll be dealing with a kind of man I've never dealt with before. You see, I know my limitations."

"You're a wise man."

"I like to think so."

"Are you also a wealthy man?"

"Wealthy? No. Can I afford you? Yes."

The other man studied Mace for a while.

"Well?" Mace asked impatiently.

"Double my usual fee."

"What?"

"Double."

"But . . . why?"

"Well, for one, because I like it here in Denver, and your job would make it necessary for me to leave."

"And second?"

The man had both of his hands tented in front of him, and now he pointed at Mace with both forefingers.

"You're going to get something out of this," he said, "something that *will* make you wealthy."

"What makes you say that?"

"I'm a student of human nature," the man said.

"You wouldn't have come all this way with two paid lackeys, and then decided to seek me out and pay my price if you didn't think you could afford it."

There was silence between them for a few moments as the two men sized each other up.

"Double," the man said.

"Done," Mace said.

"When do we start?"

"Tomorrow, I think."

"Good," the man said. "I've got a previous engagement tonight."

"I'm staying at a hotel down the street called the Douglas."

The man frowned.

"It's beneath you."

"I'm trying not to be seen. I'd like you to meet me there tomorrow morning, early."

"First light?"

Mace grimaced.

"Not that early."

"Nine?"

"That's fine."

Mace stood up.

"I'll need an . . . advance," the man said.

"I'll have it for you in the morning."

"One other thing."

"What's that?"

"The name of the man that's made it necessary for you to hire me?"

Mace frowned at the man.

"I thought you'd be older," he said.

"I will be, tomorrow," the man said. "A whole day

older, and so on, and so on. . . . The name of the man?"

"Clint Adams."

The name surprised the man, but he didn't show it. Instead he just said, "Interesting."

TWENTY-ONE

The day dragged on so that Clint started teaching Jodi how to play poker. They played in their room and when Jodi started to get bored she got an idea.

"Let's play for something."

"Do you understand the game well enough?" he asked.

"I think so."

"What do you want to play for?"

She thought a moment, then said, "Let's play for clothes."

"For clothes?" Clint asked, intrigued. "I've played for a lot of things, but never clothes. Is this something they do back East?"

"No," she said, "it's something I just thought of."

"Well, then, tell me more. How do you want to work this?"

"Whoever loses the hand has to take off an article of clothing," she said. "The loser is the first one who is totally naked."

"Doesn't sound like a loser to me," he said, "but I'm game. Do you want to deal?"

"Yes," she said. "Let's play five-card stud."

A half a dozen hands later Clint was down to his underwear and Jodi had only taken off her boots.

"This is an easy game," she said, dealing another hand while Clint shook his head.

"You're getting very good cards," he complained. Then he explained, "It's much different when you're playing for money."

"I like this game," she said.

"I can understand why."

"Oh, look, I've got an ace and you have a deuce."

"Keep dealing."

She did.

"Ooh, another ace, and you've got an eight."

He glared at her.

"You've played poker before, haven't you?"

"Of course not."

He watched her deal and could not detect any cheating—and if she wasn't cheating, how could she be getting all of these great hands?

"Three aces," she squealed, "and you've got—"

"I can see what I've got," he said, turning his cards over. "I can't beat you."

She put the deck down and clapped her hands together.

"Off with your shorts!"

Chagrined at having been beaten too easily, Clint stood up and slid his shorts down to the floor, then kicked them away.

"Ooh," she said, reaching out to touch him. "I really am the winner, aren't I?"

She got off the bed and down on her knees and began to stroke him. He began to swell in her hand.

"I love to watch it grow, don't you?" she asked, holding it in both hands.

"I never thought about it."

"It's truly an amazing thing," she said. "I hold it, or lick it . . ." She licked it to illustrate her point, and he jumped. "Or suck it . . ."

"Jesus . . ." he said as she took him deeply into her mouth.

"Mmmm," she said, sucking it wetly and then letting him pop free, fully rigid. "And it just grows. Amazing!"

"I'll show you something amazing," he said, reaching for her and pulling her to her feet.

"Like what?"

"Like how quickly I can get your clothes off *without* winning a hand of poker!"

"Oh," she said as he stripped her clothes from her body, "I think I'm going to like this game."

TWENTY-TWO

It was amazing.

Clint couldn't get a decent hand when he was playing Jodi for clothes, but that night, playing for money, he got almost nothing but decent hands. Oh, he lost with some of them, but for the most part he won.

Sitting across from him was Jefferson Baines, and to his right was Brett Garner, who was having none of the luck he'd had the last night of the tournament.

There were three other men in the game. They were Otto Herman, a businessman; Tom Lennon, a local politician; and Alan Collins who, like Baines, was simply a wealthy man. Unlike Baines, however, Collins had had his fortune handed to him when his father died.

The three local men might have liked to play poker, but they seemed to know very little about the game.

Baines was also doing well on this night, so that he and Clint were the only ones who were ahead when the game hit the three-hour mark at midnight.

"Another two hours for me, gentlemen, and no more," Clint said. "I have an early start in the morning."

"As have I," Garner said.

"Aren't you going to give us a chance to get our money back?" Otto Herman complained.

"You have two hours in which to do that, sir," Clint said, then turned his attention to Garner. "I thought you were going to stay around a few more days."

Garner took the cigar he was smoking out of his mouth and said, "Something's come up. I thought you were staying awhile."

"No," Clint said, "something's also come up for me."

It was Jeff Baines's deal, and he gave out one card down and one up, the beginnings of a five-card stud game.

"Are we playing cards?" Lennon asked.

Clint wanted to say that he was, but they didn't seem to be. He looked down and saw an ace in front of him. When he looked at his hole card, it was also an ace.

"Fifty dollars."

"On one ace?" Herman complained, but he saw the bet, even though he only had a deuce. Clint shook his head.

Baines called, as did Collins, but when it came to

Garner he said, "I'm having no luck tonight. I fold."
He turned over his king.

"You've got a king," Herman pointed out.

"So do Mr. Lennon and Mr. Baines," Garner said.
"I can't play when my cards are all over the table."

Herman frowned and seemed to be having trouble
understanding that logic—which was why he was
losing.

Collins called.

Clint took the hand with aces, and the deal passed
to Garner. Clint watched carefully as the man shuf-
fled and dealt. His physical handling of the cards was
skillful, but he wasn't playing with anywhere near
the luck or intensity of the previous week.

Clint was dealt a pair of kings this time, one up
and one down, and he mentally shook his head at
his luck. Where were these cards the other night?

He took the hand with kings and threes and the
deal passed to Collins.

The game went on that way for another hour and
a half, and by the end of that time even Baines's luck
had gone south and Clint was the only one winning.

"What a night!" Tom Lennon said, collecting the
cards while Clint raked in his pot. "It's a pleasure to
watch you play, sir."

"Thanks," Clint said, "although you *are* paying for
the privilege."

"We all are," Herman said sourly. "I find it hard to
believe you lost this week."

Clint tossed a quick glance at Baines, who
hunched his shoulders just a bit.

"Is that why you're here, Mr. Herman?" Clint
asked. "Because you thought I'd be easy pickings?"

Herman looked flustered.

"Why, uh, no," he said, "I'm just here because Jeff said there was a game with two of the, uh, best players in the tournament. After all, Mr. Garner here won, didn't he?"

"Yes, he did," Clint said.

"I was getting cards then," Garner said, "and I'm not tonight. I think this will be my last hand, gents. I'm tossing good money after bad."

As it happened he won the last hand, which did little to get him even close to even.

"I think I've had it, too," Clint said.

"We still have a half hour," Herman complained.

Clint looked at the dwindling pile of chips in front of the man.

"Are you going to get even in half an hour, Mr. Herman?"

"Well, I—"

"Are you, Mr. Lennon?"

"Not me."

Clint looked at Collins.

"Me, neither."

"I'd say the game is over, gentlemen," Jeff Baines said. "I'll cash you all out."

"I don't appreciate being dangled like bait, Jeff," Clint said as he cashed out. He had waited until the others left to cash out last.

"I'm sorry about that," Baines said, "but you've got to admit it worked out okay."

"Yeah," Clint said, accepting his money, "it worked out okay. I tell you what, Jeff."

"Yes?"

"Next time you have a tournament? Don't tell me."

"Aw, Clint—"

"Too many people knew about it from the start,

don't you think? Next time somebody might get the bright idea of hitting your game."

"With you and Bat and Ben Thompson around?"

"You better start wondering what you're going to do if it happens when Bat or Ben or I am not around, Jeff."

With that Clint turned and left the room. He found Brett Garner waiting for him outside.

"What can I do for you, Brett?"

"You were pretty hot tonight, Clint."

"I did okay."

"I thought maybe I could buy you a drink."

"I should probably buy you one."

"How about one each, then?"

"That's about all I'd have time for, Brett. I have to be up early."

"So do I," Garner said. "Two drinks. Okay?"

"Two drinks," Clint agreed.

TWENTY-THREE

Down in the bar they each got a beer—Clint paid for the first round—and walked to a back table. Garner deliberately let Clint have the chair which would put his back to the wall.

"I didn't do quite as well tonight as I did during the week," Garner observed.

"A bad run of cards," Clint said, thinking that the young man was taking the run of bad luck very well—but then he had a nice cushion from the tournament. Clint doubted that the man had dropped ten percent of what he'd won previously.

"Sort of makes us even, doesn't it?"

"Maybe," Clint said, "but there'll be other times."

Garner raised his glass and said, "To other times."

Clint drank also, wondering what Garner's reason

was for bringing him down here.

"Did you have something specific on your mind, Brett?" he asked.

"Actually, Clint," Garner said, "I was just curious about your, uh, sudden decision to leave tomorrow."

"Like you said," Clint reminded him, "something came up."

"Business?"

"Sort of," Clint said. "What about you? Business?"

Garner shrugged and said, "Sort of."

They finished their beers and Garner went to get the second round.

"Which way are you headed?" he asked when he'd brought back two fresh beers.

"Why do you ask?"

Garner shrugged and said, "Maybe we can ride a ways together."

"What if I'm taking a train?"

The man shrugged again and said, "Then I guess we couldn't ride together, could we?"

"No," Clint said, "I guess not. Which way are you headed?"

Garner hesitated, then said, "West, I'm headed west."

"Ah, see," Clint said, "I'm not."

Garner waited for Clint to tell him which way he *was* headed, and when that information wasn't forthcoming he seemed unsure what to do next.

Clint wondered why Garner was so interested in where he was going. Was he that anxious to hook up in another poker game?

"We'll end up in another game together soon enough, Brett," he said.

"Oh, I'm sure we will, Clint," the other man said,

"I'm sure we will . . . maybe even sooner than we think, huh?"

"Maybe . . ."

Clint decided not to finish the second beer.

"No offense," he said, pushing the half-finished mug away from him, "but I'm going to turn in."

"Sure, sure," Garner said, as Clint stood up. "Have a good trip."

"Yeah, you, too," Clint said.

"See you soon."

Clint waved and walked out of the bar, wondering what the hell that was all about.

When he got upstairs Jodi was in bed, but he could tell by her breathing that she was not asleep. He could also tell that she was naked. He removed his clothes and got into the bed with her, also naked. He pressed up against her so that his burgeoning cock fit right into that slot between her buttocks.

"Mmmm," she said, "you must have won."

"I did," he said, his mouth on her neck. "In fact, I was the only winner."

"See? I'm your good luck."

"How do you figure that?" he asked, running his hand up and down her thigh.

"You just have to lose to me before you go and play poker, and you'll win."

"I don't know," he said.

"Don't know what?"

"I don't know if my ego could handle losing to you all the time."

She laughed, turned over, and reached for him.

"Oh, so it's your ego you're worried about!"

• • •

Early the next morning Clint and Jodi slipped out the back door of the hotel and made their way to the hotel livery. Jodi was still complaining that she had to leave her nice clothes behind, but Clint told her that the hotel would make sure they didn't come up missing.

"Sure," she griped, "I just know some maid is going to be wearing my red dress."

When they got to the livery they were greeted by the liveryman who identified himself as Henry. It was the same man who had been there before, when they went for their ride. He was about sixty, with gray stubble that looked sharp enough to cut wood.

"William told me what you wanted, Mr. Adams," he said. "It's all ready for you."

"Good, Henry. Thanks."

They went into the livery, and Clint saw that his instructions had been carried out to the letter. Their horses were saddled, and their supplies had been separated into two burlap bags, one hanging from each of their saddles.

"Is that the way you wanted it?" Henry asked.

"That's exactly the way, Henry. Thank you."

"Do we have enough supplies?" Jodi asked. "I thought we'd have a mule, or a packhorse, or something."

"Maybe later," he said. "Right now we've got enough to get us far enough away from Denver before we have to stop again."

"Where are we headed?" she asked, as they mounted up.

He held his finger to his lips, bade Henry goodbye, and led her outside.

"I didn't want to say where we were going in front

of him," Clint said. "It seems to me the logical place to start would be Council Bluffs, Iowa."

"How long will it take us to get there?" she asked.

"I don't know," he said. "Why don't we find out?"

TWENTY-FOUR

It was almost five hundred miles from Denver to Council Bluffs, Iowa. During that time it occurred to Clint that they might already be going the route Jodi's father had taken all those years ago, but there was no way for them to know that for sure. They had no choice but to go to Council Bluffs and start back from there.

Clint knew that if he pushed hard enough they could make Council Bluffs in ten days, but he decided that there was no reason to. They took it easy, stopping twice during each day, once for a lunch rest and then overnight. During their stops he undertook Jodi's education with a gun, and with other aspects of traveling through the West on horseback.

She had told the truth about one thing. She was

an excellent horsewoman. There wasn't much he could teach her about the physical act of riding, but he did have to teach her how to ride over this terrain. . . .

"The West is very fickle," he told her. "The terrain can change from mile to mile. You've got to know what your horse can handle and what he can't. You've got to be able to see the signs that your horse needs to rest. Out here your horse is more important than anything, more important than your gun or any of your supplies. He's more important than you, because even if you get hurt your horse can take you to safety. Understand?"

"She," Jodi said.

"What?"

"My horse is a she," she said, "and yes, I understand perfectly."

"Good," he said, "*she'll* appreciate your understanding."

As for her abilities with a gun—well, she'd told the truth about that, too. The first chance they had he tested her with a rifle, and although she was far from a dead shot, she could hit what she aimed at.

She wasn't quite that good with a handgun, though.

They had not stopped in a town for the first two days, and Clint watched their back trail very carefully. When he finally felt it was safe to stop he chose a small town called North Bend, still in Colorado. It would be two more days, at least, before they crossed into Nebraska.

In North Bend they found a gun shop, and he bought her a .36 caliber Colt that fit her hand better

than either of his guns. He bought plenty of extra
rounds because he knew they'd be shooting a lot
while she was learning.

They left that town and camped earlier than usual
that night so they could use the extra daylight for her
to practice with the gun. . . .

After she had fired dozens of rounds she dropped
her arms, pointing the gun to the ground.

"It's getting heavy," she said.

"All right," he said, "enough for today."

"I don't know if I'm going to get any better, Clint,"
she said, as they sat around the fire.

"Well, to tell you the truth, Jodi," he said, "I don't
know that you have to."

"Why not?"

"What are you planning to do after we find your
father's grave?"

"I don't know."

"Well, unless you're going to stay in the West and
travel a lot on horseback, you really won't need to
get much better with a handgun. Right now I think
you'd be able to hit a man in the chest from five feet
away, and that might be good enough."

"What if we run into Indians?"

"Not much chance of that," he said. "The Sioux
are on the reservation, and they haven't been much
of a problem in these parts since Crazy Horse was
killed."

"Well then," she said, "I guess I'll have to decide
what I'm going to do, won't I?"

"I guess you will."

·   ·   ·

The other problem they had was her reaction to the sun. After one day of riding, her skin was red and painful. That night he fried up some bacon and applied the grease to her skin.

"It hurts," she said. "It feels like it's going to tear."

"The grease should make it feel less tight," he said. "Haven't you ever had sunburn before?"

"Not like this."

"You'll be used to it in a few days," he said. "It won't hurt forever."

"Can't I keep covered up? Like with a long-sleeved shirt?"

"You'll melt in a long-sleeved shirt, Jodi," he said. "The only way to beat the sun is to get used to it. Before long your skin won't be red, it'll be brown."

"That doesn't sound attractive."

He smiled and said, "That depends on how you look at it."

"What do you mean?"

"Well, it'll make the parts of your body that the sun isn't getting to even more interesting, don't you think?"

TWENTY-FIVE

They made Council Bluffs in two weeks, and even though Clint hadn't pushed their progress Jodi was pretty much worn-out by the time they arrived.

Clint had never been to Council Bluffs before, although he'd been to Omaha, which was right over the border. Consequently, he knew no one in town who could help them.

At the livery, after they'd given up their horses, she asked, "What do we do now that we're here?"

"Well," he said, "first we get a hotel room, and then a meal. After that we get some rest, and then maybe we'll talk about our next move."

"I'm all right," she said, even as she staggered from her fatigue.

"Yeah, I know," he said, "but I'm tired. Come on, let's find the nearest hotel."

From a front window on the second floor of his hotel, the man called Mace looked down at the main street.

"Son of a bitch!" he swore.

"What is it?" Dennis Pelter asked.

"He was right," Mace said, watching Clint and Jodi Benton walk down the street. They were heading toward Council Bluffs' other hotel, which was right across the street.

"They're here?" Pelter asked.

"See for yourself," Mace said.

Pelter moved to the window and looked out.

"Okay," Pelter said, "so he was right. I still don't think we need him."

"He said they'd have to come here to start," Mace said. He was talking about the man he'd hired in Denver. When Pelter and Sullivan discovered that Mace had hired another man they had complained. "And he knew how to get us here ahead of them."

Pelter moved away from the window and sat down on one of the room's two beds. He and Mace were sharing a room, while Sullivan had to share a room with the new man.

"Okay, so he came in handy this far," he said. "Now we can get rid of him."

Mace turned and stared at Pelter.

"Since when did you start calling the shots here?" he demanded.

"I ain't tryin' to call the shots," Pelter said, "I'm just sayin'—"

"Well, don't say, Dennis!" Mace snapped. "I do the

saying, and you do the listening. Understand?"

"Sure, Mace, sure," Pelter said. "I'm just tryin' to save you money."

"It's my money," Mace said, "and I'll spend it as I see fit."

"Sure, sure . . ." Pelter said, shrinking back from Mace's anger.

Mace turned and looked out the window again.

"Go and get him," he said. "Tell him I want to talk to him."

"Yeah," Pelter said, "right." He welcomed the opportunity to get out of the room. He'd send the man back on his own. He wanted to stay away from Mace until he cooled off.

As Pelter left the room, Mace was thinking more and more that if there was anyone who wasn't needed it was Pelter and Sullivan. He and the new man could probably handle this themselves, and *that* would be saving money. He didn't want the others to know about it, but that *was* a consideration. Until he found what he was looking for he was operating on his own funds, and they were anything but limitless. He'd sunk his entire worth into this project, and he couldn't afford to have it fail.

But from the way things were looking, it wasn't going to.

TWENTY-SIX

Clint and Jodi registered in the Three Star Hotel, across the street from the Bluffs House Hotel, for no other reason than that Clint liked the name better. From the outside one seemed as good as the other.

"One room?" he asked Jodi as they entered.

"Of course," she said, and then added, "after all, I am paying."

"Right," he said, as if that was the reason, "we'll save money that way."

"Right."

They checked in and carried their own gear upstairs.

"I need a bath," she said.

"Let's eat first," he said, "then you can bathe and go right to sleep."

"What about you?"

"I'm going to start asking around and see what I can find out about the wagon trains."

"I thought you said you were tired."

"I am," he said, "but you're exhausted."

She decided she couldn't argue with that.

"Okay," she said, "you win. Let's eat."

They went downstairs, and Clint asked the desk clerk for a good place to eat.

"There's plenty of them up and down the street," the young man said. "All I can tell you is, don't eat here."

"Thanks for the warning."

"Don't mention it," the man said, looking Jodi up and down.

She looked a lot different from the Jodi Benton who had left Denver, Colorado, two weeks earlier. She had lost some weight, but seemed to have lost it in her waist, so that her breasts were accentuated even more. Also, her once pale skin was now nut-brown, which went well with her dark hair.

"You could be an Indian, if I didn't know better," Clint had said at one point.

"Is that good?"

"I've known some beautiful Indian women," Clint said. "Yes, that's good."

Now they left the hotel lobby, turned right, and started walking. They stopped in the first café they came to and found that the clerk had been right. The food was delicious—either that, or they were very hungry.

After they had eaten, Jodi's eyes started to close at the table.

"Come on," he said, "let's get you back to the hotel. Maybe we should change the order of things to do."

"What do you mean?" she asked, stifling a yawn.

"Maybe you should sleep first," he said, "and then take a bath."

"Whatever you say," she replied. "You're the boss."

"I'm going to remind you that you said that."

From the window across the street, two men watched as Clint and Jodi walked back to their hotel.

"There they are," Mace said, "just like you said they would be."

The other man looked at him.

"I just made an educated guess based on what you told me."

"It was more than a guess," Mace said. "It had to be, or I wouldn't have come here with you."

"It *was* more than a guess," the man said.

"Well, good, because I——"

"It was an *educated* guess," the man said, cutting him off, "and those are usually right."

"Jesus," Mace said, "we could have lost them if you were wrong."

"But I wasn't wrong," the man said, "was I?"

"No," Mace said, after a moment, "no, you weren't."

The man walked away from the window and sat down on the bed.

"You're not paying me to be wrong."

"No, I'm not," Mace said. "So what's your next educated guess?"

"They'll need some rest," the man said, "even

though they didn't push as hard to get here as we did."

Mace and the others had been in Council Bluffs for three days already. He *had* been starting to worry.

"And then?"

"And then Adams will start asking around town for anyone with a memory twenty years long."

"And if he doesn't find someone?"

"Oh, he will."

"How can you be so sure?" Mace asked. "Oh, wait, another educated guess?"

"No," the man said, "these towns always have someone with a memory that long."

"Then why don't we find them?"

"Because you told me you wanted to follow the woman," the man said. "If you wanted to cut her out and go it on your own, you should have told me that."

"And then what?"

"Then she'd have to be killed."

"And what about Adams?"

"Him, too," the man said, "unless you wanted to try to buy him off."

"Could he be bought?"

The man hesitated, then said, "In my experience? Not a chance."

"Could you kill him?" Mace asked. "I mean, if I wanted you to?"

"Anybody can be killed, Mace."

"That means you could?"

"If you paid me enough."

More money, Mace thought.

"No," he said then, "no, I think we'll let them do the work and follow them."

"Then I have a suggestion."

"And what's that?"

"That you and I follow them," the man said, "while Sullivan and Pelter follow us."

"Why?"

"Because if the four of us try to follow them, Adams will spot us."

"And he won't spot you and me?"

"He might," the man said. "He wouldn't spot me, but he might spot both of us. That's a chance we'll have to take, though . . . that is, unless you want me to go on alone?"

"No," Mace said, "I'm coming along. I want to be there when she finds it."

"Finds what?" the man asked. "You still haven't told me."

"That's right," Mace said, "I haven't."

The two men matched stares and then the other man said, "Suit yourself. As long as you pay me, I don't have to know."

"Don't worry," Mace said. "As long as you keep producing like this, I'll keep paying you."

TWENTY-SEVEN

Clint allowed Jodi to fall on the bed fully dressed and covered her with a blanket. She was fast asleep before he could leave the room.

Clint knew very little about Council Bluffs, so he went to the office of the *Council Bluffs Journal*, the local newspaper, to get the information he needed.

The editor of the paper set him up at a table with back issues. The man's filing system was so good that he was able to produce issues that talked about Council Bluffs as a "jumping off" place for wagon trains that were headed to Oregon or California. According to Jodi, her father had only wanted to go as far as Colorado.

In reading the newspaper Clint discovered that many small towns along the Missouri River were jumping off places, towns like Council Bluffs, St. Joseph, and Independence. Often people would winter there, waiting until the snow and ice melted in April to cross the Missouri and begin their trek west. Of course, the newspapers couldn't tell Clint anything about Jodi's father, Henry Benton.

The newspaper editor was a young man, probably not yet thirty, which surprised Clint.

"It's no surprise," Brendan Murphy said. "My father started the newspaper forty years ago. I took it over when he died five years ago."

"Are any of your father's friends or colleagues still around?" Clint asked.

"Sure," Murphy said. "Why?"

"I'm looking to locate the whereabouts of a man named Henry Benton, who came here about twenty years ago and left with a wagon train."

"Where was he headed?"

"Denver."

"You sure he didn't go by stagecoach?" Murphy asked.

"Stagecoach?"

Murphy nodded.

"Right around 1863 stagecoaches started going to Denver from here and some other places, like Atchison, Kansas. I know some folks who traveled by coach from Atchison to Denver—that's *seven hundred miles*—and made it in seven days by traveling twenty-four hours."

"That's interesting," Clint said, "but I'm almost certain this man went by wagon train. Would there be anyone in town who might remember that time?"

"Sure, sure," Murphy said, "but how about letting

me come along with you when you talk to them?"

"Why?"

"Well, for one thing, there might be a human interest story in it for me."

"I don't think—"

"And for another," the newspaperman went on, "they won't talk to you because you're a stranger."

Clint stared at the man.

"They're old," Murphy said with a shrug, as if that explained everything.

Clint thought a moment, then said, "Okay."

"I'll get my hat. . . ."

"What did you say your name was?" Murphy asked, pencil poised over a pad as he struggled to match the longer strides of Clint Adams.

"I didn't say."

After a few moments the editor asked, "Well, what is it?"

"It's not important," Clint said.

"Why not?"

"I don't want it in the newspaper." As soon as he said it he regretted it. Why couldn't he have just lied and given another name? All he'd done now was pique the editor's interest.

"Whoa, you must be somebody famous, then."

"Not so famous."

"Okay, well-known. You figure if your name appears in my paper it would be recognized?"

"Mr. Murphy," Clint said, "I brought you along to introduce me, not to interview me."

"Hey, you can't blame a guy for tryin', can you?" the man asked.

"No," Clint said, "I guess not."

They walked along a few more yards and then Murphy asked, "So what did you say your name was?"

TWENTY-EIGHT

Murphy said there were three men he could think of who were old enough to remember the wagon train activity in Council Bluffs twenty years ago but not so old that they *couldn't* remember it.

The first was Ol' Jesse Williams. Williams was eighty-three and "sharp as a tack," according to Murphy.

"Where do we find this Williams?"

"Where else?" Murphy said. "The saloon."

"Is he a drunk?"

"Hell no," Murphy said. "I don't even think he drinks much anymore. He sits in the saloon and talks to people, always has a shot glass full of whiskey in front of him."

"I thought you said he wasn't a drunk."

111

"He ain't," Murphy said. "He keeps the *same* glass of whiskey in front him. I think he tosses it off at night before he leaves to turn in."

"That's his whole life now?" Clint asked. "Just sitting in the saloon?"

"Well, he's had a pretty full and active life."

"What did he do for a living?"

"Well," Murphy said, "up until eight years ago, when the town made him retire at seventy-five, Jesse Williams was the sheriff of Council Bluffs."

As it turned out, Williams was the sheriff of Council Bluffs for better than thirty-years until the town finally decided to put him out to pasture. He now lived rent-free in a house at the end of town, and never had to pay for his meals or his drinks—or *drink*.

As Brendan Murphy had said, they found Jesse Williams sitting in the saloon with a drink in front of him, only he wasn't talking to anyone.

Standing just inside the door Murphy said, "Actually, folks tend to stay away from Ol' Jesse these days, or else he'll talk their ears off."

Suddenly, Clint's opinion about the town changed. He'd thought it damned decent of them to give the old sheriff a place to live and not charge him for his meals, but now that seemed to be in lieu of talking to the man. Clint wondered how Jesse Williams would choose, were he given the choice. A place to live, or somebody to talk to?

"Are you going to introduce me?" Clint asked.

"Well, uh, no."

"Why not?"

"Well . . . Jesse and my father were friends, but he's never liked me."

"You told me he wouldn't talk to me without you."

"I lied."

Clint stared at him.

"Well, I thought there might be a story in you," Murphy said. "In fact, I still do."

"Thanks for your help, Mr. Murphy."

"The other two I told you about—Ed Woodsen and Jimmy Key—they won't talk to you without me."

"Yeah . . ."

"They won't!"

"I'll take my chances," Clint said. "Good-bye, Mr. Murphy."

"But—"

Clint wasn't listening, though. He was walking across the room to where Jesse Williams was sitting. He noticed that the man still wore a gun around his hip, an old but well cared for Colt.

"Sheriff Williams?"

The old man turned his head and looked up at Clint. He wasn't heavy, but he had a second chin hanging beneath the first one. His eyes were blue but sort of filmy—they were intelligent, though. The light behind them hadn't gone out completely.

"Nobody's called me that for years," the old man said.

"Well, they should," Clint said. "It's a damned shame, if you ask me, the way this town treats a man who was their sheriff for more than thirty years."

"You got that right," Williams said. "Put me out to pasture and give me a house and they think that's all I need."

"A man needs company."

"He sure does," Williams said. "Somebody to talk to."

"You mind if I get a beer and sit with you for a spell, sir?"

"Nobody's called me that, either," Williams said. "Sure, young feller, have a seat. I gotta warn ya, though."

"About what?"

"Once I start talkin' I might not stop."

"I'll take my chances, sir."

"All right, then," Williams said. "Go and get that beer and tell the bartender it's on my tab."

Even though Clint knew the man didn't pay for his drinks, he counted that as a generous offer.

"I'll do that, sir."

Clint walked to the bar.

"Let me have a beer, please."

"Comin' up," the bartender said.

He turned and placed the beer in front of him.

"How much?" Clint asked.

"Nothin'," the bartender said. "I heard Jesse say it was on his tab."

Clint leaned forward and said to the man, "But he doesn't pay for his drinks, anyway."

The bartender, a gray-haired man in his fifties, said in a low voice, "I'll tell you a secret, friend. Even if the town hadn't voted to give him his food and drink for nothin', I would never charge Jesse. He gave almost his whole life to this town. I'm the only one ever exchanges ten words with him every day. It's a cryin' shame."

"It sure is," Clint said. "Thanks for the beer."

"You got as many of those as you want, friend,"

the bartender said, "long as they're on Jesse."

Clint walked back to Jesse's table, thinking that maybe there was one decent person in this town, after all.

TWENTY-NINE

Clint sat with Jesse Williams for an hour, just letting the old man ramble on. Eventually, the man got back to the time period Clint was interested in, and he started asking him questions.

"That was durin' the War," Jesse said, "and people was still movin' west as fast as they could. I think some of them thought the War couldn't catch up with them out there.

"That War," he said, shaking his head. "I woulda went, ya know, but even then I was old. In my sixties, I was."

"Young enough to keep your sheriff's job," Clint said.

"Ah," Jesse said, waving his hand, "maybe that was a rough job in the forties and fifties, but the last fifteen years I wore that badge I never had to struggle none. A few drunks, maybe, shootin' up the town, but that was it. Ya know, Clay Allison came to town once, but he was no trouble. No trouble at all."

"Maybe he didn't want to tangle with you."

Jesse looked across the table at Clint and then started to cackle.

"I say something funny?" Clint asked.

"Son," Jesse said, "you been real good, truly you have. You been listenin' to Ol' Jesse ramble on and on, and you been sayin' the right things."

"I don't understand."

"Well, I may be old and my body may be some feeble, but my brain ain't rotted out yet. What're you after, son?"

"After?"

"Come on, come on, don't put an old man on," Jesse said. "There's some piece of information that you're after that you think Ol' Jesse can give you. Who brung you here?"

Clint decided to tell the truth.

"Brendan Murphy."

"That little weasel!" Jesse said, with distaste. "He ain't a pimple on his daddy's ass, that boy. Where is he?"

"I sent him packing, Jesse."

"Why?"

"He lied to me," Clint said. "He told me you and some others wouldn't talk to me if he wasn't around."

"What others?"

Clint dug the names out of his mind.

"Um, Jimmy Key and Ed Woodsen."

"Huh," Jesse said, "ain't none of us would cross

the street to piss on that boy if he was on fire."

"I didn't think he was that bad."

"He not only lies, he lies in print. He puts whatever he thinks will sell newspapers into the *Journal*. His daddy built that paper and never printed an untrue word the whole time he was editor. Naw." Jesse said, shaking his head, "I'd crap square and in the colors of the rainbow before I'd help him or any friend of his." Jesse eyed Clint warily. "Sent him packin', ya say?"

"I don't like liars."

Jesse studied Clint for a few moments, then laughed and said, "Yeah, ya know how to say the right things, all right. What's your name, son?"

"Does that matter?"

"It does if ya want to ask me some question. What's your name?"

"Clint Adams."

Jesse sat back in his chair and stared at Clint for a few minutes. Then he did something that surprised Clint. The shot glass of whiskey had been in front of the old man this whole time. Murphy hadn't lied about that. But the old man picked it up now and tossed it off, setting the glass down with a bang.

"Another one, Benny!"

The look of surprise on the bartender's face told Clint that Murphy hadn't been lying about the drink. Benny was shocked that Jesse wanted a second one.

"Another one, Jesse?"

"That's right, another one!" the old man shouted. "Jesus Christ, can't a man have a second drink around here?"

"Sure, Jesse, sure," the bartender said. The man hurried over with a bottle and poured a second drink for the ex-lawman. "You want me to leave the bottle, Jesse?"

"Jesus Christ, man, ya tryin' ta kill me? Two drinks is enough!"

The second drink was in front of Jesse, and he ignored it and looked at Clint.

"Why didn't ya tell me right off who ya was?" he demanded.

Clint shrugged.

"I didn't think it mattered."

"Hell, man, ya used ta wear a badge, too."

"That was a long time ago, Jesse."

"Don't matter," Jesse said, shaking his head so that his second chin wobbled, "we both used ta wear the tin, and that means I got ta help ya if I can, so, Mr. Adams, ya go ahead and ask me what ya got ta ask me, and I'll answer if I can."

"Are you hungry, Jesse?" Clint asked.

"I could eat," Jesse said, "but ya got ta let me buy ya dinner. Hell, you're a guest in my town."

Clint had forgotten that Jesse's meals were on the house, too.

"Where can we go to eat?" Clint asked.

"Right here," Jesse said. "Benny makes the best steaks in town—ain't that right, Benny?"

"That's right, Jesse."

"Then get two of 'em goin', man," Jesse said, "while I still got enough teeth left to eat one."

THIRTY

"Henry Benton, ya say?"

"That's right."

Jesse thought the name over while he put his few teeth to work on a piece of meat. Clint wondered when the last time was that Jesse had had steak, because Benny certainly did not make the best steak Clint had ever tasted. If this was the best steak in town—overdone and tough as old gravy—then Clint felt sorry for the people of Council Bluffs.

"Can't say as the name rings a bell," Jesse said finally.

"It would have been sixty-two, probably just before April." Clint had gotten this from Jodi during their trip. The timetable she gave him would have put her father here just before the thaw.

"If he was here in March he woulda had ta stay in a hotel, or boardinghouse," Jesse said. "There were lots of them then, but most of them are gone."

"What about the people who owned them?"

"Gone."

"Somebody who worked there?"

"Gone."

Clint had the feeling that to Jesse "gone" and "dead" meant the same thing.

"Jesse," Clint asked, "who would be around who might know something?"

"Well, we got a stage office here that used ta run the wagon train."

"And what happened?"

"Well, why travel by wagon train when you can travel by train?" Jesse said. "Now they just run a stage."

"But would they have any records from twenty years ago?"

"They might."

"Who would I ask?"

"Well, I guess you'd ask whoever's runnin' the place now . . ."

"And that would be?"

"Ol' Harve Anderson's boy Steve."

"Steve Anderson."

"Yeah, but Steve's real young and not worth the spit his daddy used ta shine his boots."

Clint was getting the feeling that Jesse didn't have much respect for Council Bluffs' younger population.

"Well, he'd know where the records were, wouldn't he?" Clint asked.

"I wouldn't count on that none."

"Then who would?"

"Well, young Brendan wasn't tellin' you no lie when he gave you Jimmy Key's name," Jesse said. "Ol' Jimmy was workin' for the line back then."

"So he'd know where the records were?"

"I guess so," Jesse said, "or he might jest remember somethin' that I don't, since he was involved in filling those wagon trains up."

"And where can I find Jimmy Key?"

"He works at the livery."

"I guess they didn't put him out to pasture yet, huh?" Clint asked.

"Hell, no," Jesse said, "why would they? Jimmy's a youngster."

"A youngster?" Clint asked. "Just how old is he?"

"Hell, he can't be more'n . . . seventy-four."

"Uh-huh," Clint said.

Clint thanked Jesse for the information and the meal.

"Hell, son," Jesse said, "thanks for the conversation."

When Clint left Jesse he was sitting with that second drink still in front of him.

He walked over to the livery and found an old man sitting there on a bale of hay, smoking a cigarette.

"Isn't that a little dangerous?" he asked.

The man looked down at the bale he was sitting on, then up at Clint.

"Why?"

"Might start a fire."

"So I burn up and don't make seventy-five?" the man said. "Big deal. What can I do fer you, young feller?"

"Jesse sent me over."

"Jesse?" the man asked. "Sent you to see me?"

"He did if you're Jimmy Key."

"I'm Jimmy," the man said. "You talked to Jesse?"

"I sure did."

"An' you got hearing left?"

"He wasn't so bad."

"Why'd you talk to Jesse?"

"I'm trying to find out about a man who was in town twenty years ago to take a wagon train west."

"Hell," Key said, "there was lots of 'em."

"I know," Clint said. "I've got a name. Jesse thought you might be able to help me because you worked for the company that ran the wagon train back then."

"What's the name?"

"Benton, Henry Benton."

"Benton . . ." Key repeated. "You sure you don't mean Benson? Knew a Harry Benson."

"It was Benton," Clint said again, "Henry Benton. Came here from Philadelphia. He was interested in going only as far as Denver."

"Benton," Key said again, shaking his head, "naw, I don't remember the name."

"I wonder if you can tell me, were there records of the passengers back then?"

"Records? Oh, you mean the names?"

"Yes, that's what I mean."

"Well, sure there was," Key said. "We was runnin' a business, wasn't we?"

"Yes, I guess you were. Tell me, Jimmy—can I call you Jimmy?"

"I'm seventy-four years old, young fella," Jimmy

Key said. "If'n I didn't want you to call me Jimmy, how would I stop ya?"

"Well," Clint said, "if you didn't want me to call you Jimmy, I wouldn't."

"Jus' like that, huh?"

"Just like that," Clint said.

The old man thought about that for a while, then dropped his cigarette to the dirt floor and crushed it with his boot toe.

"Naw," he said, "that's okay, you kin call me Jimmy."

"Okay, Jimmy," Clint said, "tell me, would you know where those records were?"

Key hesitated, then said, "I might."

"Could you help me find them?"

"I might."

"Uh, when would you decide if you will or won't?" Clint asked.

"What did you give Ol' Jesse?"

"Nothing," Clint said. "He bought me a drink and a meal."

Key made a rude sound with his mouth.

"He don't pay for none of those things, anyway," he said. "Some of us ain't that lucky."

"Well, what would you want, Jimmy? Money?"

"Money would be nice."

"Well," Clint said, "if I was to find the information I'm looking for, I think a finder's fee would be in order."

"A what?"

"Money, Jimmy."

"Well, whyn't ya say so?" the old man said, standing up from the hay bale. "Come on, we're wastin' time."

THIRTY-ONE

"What are you doin' here?" a man asked as Jimmy Key and Clint walked into the office of the Council Bluffs Stage & Freight Line.

"Don't get all crazy on me, Stevie," Key said. "Man here needs some information from your records."

"Hey, Jimmy," Steve Anderson said, putting his hands on his hips in an impatient gesture, "you can't just come in here—"

"You forgit, Stevie boy," Key said, "I still own a piece of this place."

That surprised Clint.

Anderson, a tall, blond man in his early thirties, had a face that seemed to be set in a perpetual pout.

"Yeah, but you said you'd keep your nose out of operations—"

"I ain't stickin' my nose in your operation, Steve,"
Key said. "We're just gonna go out back and look for
some old records from twenty years ago."

"Well . . . as long as you stay out back."

"Yeah, yeah . . ." Key said. "Come on."

Key led Clint through a door that led into what
looked like a big warehouse. It was filled with items
people were shipping either east or west, including
furniture. Clint saw tables and chairs and trunks all
around as they walked through the place. Finally
they reached a dingy back room that was filled with
boxes. Key lit a lamp that bathed the room in an
unpleasant yellow light.

"These are the records."

"I have to go through all of these?" Clint asked.
"That's impossible."

"Not all of it," Key said. "I can find the boxes for
early 1862—if you're sure that was the year your man
was here."

"That's the year I have."

"Okay, then," Key said, "let's have a look. . . ."

Hours later Clint was studying the names of the
passengers on the wagon trains that left Council
Bluffs in April of '62. As it turned out, Key hadn't
remembered exactly where the records were. In fact,
Clint was starting to worry that the old man was
imagining things when they finally found the records
that he wanted.

"Now I get paid, right?" Key asked. "It don't matter
if you find his name or not?"

"I'll pay you," Clint said, but he was wondering
how much you paid somebody who owned a piece
of a freight line. "How come you don't have any con-

trol here, Jimmy, if you own a piece of the line?"

"Ah, I only own a small piece because Stevie's father put me in his will. He said I had to be a part of the business as long as I was alive." He cackled. "Hell, even if Stevie sold the line I'd have to go with it. Ain't that a kick?"

"It sure is," Clint said, studying long lists of names that seemed to stretch on forever. He had no idea that there were wagon trains of this size back then. "Jimmy, can I take these lists with me?"

Key squinted suspiciously.

"Where?"

"Just to my hotel so Benton's daughter can help me look for his name."

Key thought it over for a few moments then said, "Ah, why not? It'd probably burn Stevie's butt if he found out about it. You won't tell him, will ya?"

"No, I won't tell him."

"Good," Key said, cackling, "that means I can. I love gettin' that young pup mad."

Clint gathered up the lists and shoved them inside his shirt. Now that he knew that Key owned only a token piece of the line he didn't want Steve Anderson to see him taking anything out of the place.

They put the boxes back in place and Clint said, "Okay, let's go."

THIRTY-TWO

When Clint returned to the hotel, Jodi was awake and waiting for him.

"Where have you been?" she asked anxiously. She still looked tired.

"I was out getting these," he said, brandishing the papers in his hands.

"What are those?"

"Lists," he said, "of people who traveled on wagon trains from here to . . . well, to wherever they were going."

"When?"

"Early in 1862."

"Is my father's name there?"

"I don't know," he said. "I haven't had time to look. I thought we'd look together."

She stood up from the bed, where she'd been sitting. Her look had changed from anxious to excited.

"What are we waiting for?"

For an hour they scanned the lists, until Clint's eyes burned.

"Anything?" he asked.

"No," she said, "nothing. I don't understand."

"Is your information good, Jodi?"

"I hope so."

"Where did you get it?"

"From my mother."

"But I thought your mother died when you were young," Clint said.

"I got the information from a friend of hers," Jodi said, "a woman who knew both my mother and my father. *She* gave me the information that she could, which she had heard from my mother—"

"So this is secondhand material?"

"Yes."

"But you trust it?"

"Yes."

"Well," Clint said, spreading his hands helplessly, "if your father's not on this list—"

"That doesn't mean he wasn't on one of the wagon trains."

"How do you figure that?"

"He could have sneaked on—"

"I don't think—"

"Or he could have gotten on under a different name."

Clint stared at her.

"What haven't you been telling me?"

Jodi hesitated, then stood up—they'd been sitting

on the bed with the lists—and walked to the window.

"My father was . . . running from the law."

"For what?"

"I'm not even sure," she said. "I haven't been able to piece together the whole story. All I know is that the police were after him, so he might have been traveling under an assumed name."

Clint opened his hands and the sheets of paper he'd been holding fluttered to the floor.

"Then these aren't going to do us much good, are they?" he asked.

"I don't know," she said. "Maybe I can look again. Maybe I'll recognize the name he used."

"What are the chances of that?"

"I don't know," she said, walking to the bed again. "Maybe he used a friend's name, or a relative's."

"All right," Clint said. "You do that, then."

"What are you going to do?"

"There's another man in town I could talk to," he said, strapping his gun back on. He'd taken it off when they sat down to go through the lists. "I'll see if I can find him. Maybe he'll remember something."

"All right."

"I'll be back in a while."

She walked to him and kissed him on the lips lightly.

"Thank you."

"Thank me after we find him."

"I will," she said, "and that will be for finding him. Now I'm just thanking you for trying."

"Well . . . you're welcome," he said, and went out the door.

*   *   *

From the hotel across the street, Mace watched Clint Adams leave his hotel.

"I'll be back," he said to the man in the room with him.

"Where are you going?"

"I've got to talk to Jodi."

"Do you think that's wise?"

"She's afraid of me," Mace said. "I want her to know I'm here."

"Don't you think she'll tell Adams?"

"She won't want him to know that she's been lying to him," Mace said. "I think she'll keep quiet. Besides, she thinks she can handle me."

"You mean," the man asked, "she's afraid of you but she doesn't know it?"

"Something like that," Mace said. "It's a complicated relationship."

"I better come with you," the man said.

"What for?"

"To watch your back. Adams might come back right away."

"I won't take long with her," Mace said, "I just want her to know I'm here . . . but okay, come along. Maybe it's not such a bad idea."

THIRTY-THREE

Clint remembered the third name Murphy had given him—Ed Woodsen—but he didn't know where to find the man. He went to the saloon to see if Jesse Williams was there, but he wasn't. The saloon was busier than before, and there were other men sitting at Jesse's table. Clint went to the bar.

"Back again?" the bartender asked.

"I'm looking for Jesse."

"He went home."

"Can you tell me where he lives?"

"I can, but it won't do you any good."

"Why not?"

"Once Jesse goes home he goes to bed, and once he does that he's no good to anybody until morning."

"Wouldn't I be able to wake him up just to talk to him for a few minutes?"

"You could try," the man said, "but I don't think he'd make much sense."

Clint took the location of Jesse's house from the man, but decided to try Jimmy Key before he tried the old lawman.

He found Key at the livery, sitting on the same bale of hay.

"You come to pay me?" Key asked.

Clint had forgotten about that.

"How much do you want?"

Key thought about it a few moments, then surprised Clint with his answer.

"Ten bucks."

"Is that all?" Clint asked. "I thought you'd want more."

Key shrugged.

"It's the principle of the thing," he said. "I don't really need the money, but I don't like giving away information for free."

"Okay," Clint said, "ten dollars it is."

He handed the man the money, and Key pocketed it.

"What can I do for you now?"

"I'm looking for Ed Woodsen."

"What for?"

"I want to ask him some questions."

"About the same thing? That feller you're lookin' for?"

Clint nodded.

"He's gonna make you pay him more than I did."

"Does he know anything?"

"He might," Key answered. "Ed used to work the trains back then."

"Work them?"

"Rode along with them. Scouted for 'em."

"Was he ever a train master?"

"Naw," Key said, "only special fellers got hired for that. He was a scout sometimes, and a hand most of the times."

"And how old is Woodsen?"

"Ed? Oh, he must be about . . . my age, I guess."

"So he wouldn't be asleep now?"

"Oh, you heard about Jesse goin' to sleep, huh?"

"I heard."

"Sleeps like the dead, he does, but then he's eighty . . . something."

"Three."

"Yeah, that's right, three."

"Can you take me to Woodsen, Jimmy?"

"Sure, sure, I can take you to Ed."

"Do I have to pay you?"

"Naw," Key said, waving his hand, "not just to take you to 'im."

"Where is he?"

"There's a couple of places he could be," Key said, "but my money's on the whorehouse, Katie's place."

"But I thought you said he was . . ." Clint trailed off, realizing that questioning Ed Woodsen's virility at seventy-four would also be questioning Jimmy Key's.

"Hey," Key said, "we may be old, but we ain't dead."

THIRTY-FOUR

As Jimmy Key had suspected, Ed Woodsen was at the whorehouse.

"Who's your friend?" the madame asked. She was in her sixties, and her face was covered with powder and rouge. What was once a handsome body had gone to fat and was corseted and cinched to no avail.

"Katie, this here is . . . Clint," Key said, deciding not to use Clint's last name. "We're lookin' for Ed Woodsen. Is he here?"

"He sure is," Katie said. "He's with Lola." Katie looked at Clint and added, "Lola's my oldest whore, and she's still thirty years younger than the old goat."

"Lola's a damn good whore," Jimmy Key said.

"She used to be," Katie said, "but now you and old Ed are the only ones who ask for her."

"How long has he been with her?" Clint asked.

" 'Bout an hour," she said.

"Then he's almost done?"

"Are you kiddin'?" Katie asked. "It takes that long for the old goat to get goin'."

"Katie!" Key said, his tone scolding.

"Well, it does," Katie said. "Maybe you can still get hard faster than that, but old Ed can't."

"He's the same age as me."

"So maybe you can't get hard neither," the old whore said.

"You wanna try me?" Key demanded. "You ain't been with a man in so long—"

"You watch how you talk to me in my place, Jimmy Key,—" she snapped.

"Could we hold it a minute?" Clint asked. "Before you two get into a knock-down-drag-out brawl, when will Woodsen be finished?"

"Well," she said, glaring at Key, "once these old birds get hard they shoot their loads pretty quick. He'll probably be down any minute."

"Is it okay if I wait?" Clint asked.

Now Katie looked at him like he was a potential customer, and forgot all about her anger—if it was ever truly genuine. Clint had the feeling that Key and Katie went through this more times than not.

"Sure, you can wait, sugar," she said, taking his arm. "Come into the parlor."

She looked past him at the old man and said, "You get out of here, Jimmy Key."

"I got work to do, anyways," Key said. "You gonna be okay in here, young feller?"

Before Clint could answer Katie said, "Sure he is,

Jimmy. Me and the girls are gonna take real good care of him."

As Key left she led Clint into the parlor, which was filled with girls and women in various stages of dress . . . and undress.

"It's a little early for most of the men in town," she explained. "They usually wait until after dark so their wives can't see them comin' in here."

"Makes sense to me," Clint said.

"I guess that gives you your pick, sugar," she said. "See anything that suits your fancy?"

The truth of the matter was he hardly saw anything that *didn't* strike his fancy, but with Jodi waiting back in the room he didn't feel that going upstairs with one of these soiled doves was the thing to do.

"Take your time, lover," Katie said. "Look 'em over good."

Clint felt that if he did just that, took his time looking them over, maybe Woodsen would come down and he'd be saved from having to make a choice—or not.

There were easily a dozen women in the room, and the scent of their different perfumes was almost cloying. He thought that it would have made more sense for all of them to wear the same scent.

They all wore different outfits, though, and that was okay with him. One outfit revealed as much—or more—than another.

One girl was young and blond and very slender, with hardly a curve of hip or breast, but she had the prettiest face and the smoothest, whitest skin. . . .

Another woman, older but only in her late twenties, wore a corset and filmy thing that revealed most of her impressive bosom, including the pink crescent of each aureola. . . .

There was a black woman there, mid-twenties or so, tall and full-hipped. She turned sideways to show him her impressive butt, as well. . . .

There were breasts of all sizes and shapes, from cannonballs to peaches, soft ones, hard ones, pointing ones and round ones. . . .

Legs: long ones and short ones, slender thighs and full ones. . . .

Dark skin, light skin, long hair, short hair, blond, brunette, redhead, and some shades that Clint couldn't quite identify.

"Quite a choice, eh?" Katie asked.

"To say the least," Clint said.

"Well, then, go ahead, honey," she said, "pick one. . . ."

All the girls posed, showing him their best features. Breasts were thrust at him, hips were shot out, toes were pointed to show off legs. If not for Jodi, he might have picked the big-breasted blonde, or the tall black woman . . . hmm, the chunky redhead looked interesting. . . .

But he wasn't here for that.

"Ma'am," he said to Katie, "your girls are all beautiful." He looked at the women and added, "You truly are." Then he looked back at Katie. "But I really didn't come here for this. I just came to talk to Ed Woodsen."

Suddenly he heard someone on the stairs behind him and a voice called out, "Did I hear somebody say my name?"

THIRTY-FIVE

When the knock sounded on the door, Jodi assumed it was Clint. She left the lists on the bed and went to open the door. When she saw who it was, she caught her breath.

"Hello, kitten," Mace said.

"What the hell are you doing here?" she asked Roger Mason, her ex-husband.

"I just wanted to talk to you, that's all."

"How did you find me?"

"It wasn't hard."

"You can't be here."

"Why not?" he asked. "Your boyfriend left. I saw him go."

"He's not my boyfriend," she said. "You can't be here, Roger."

"Sure I can."

"Do you know who he is?"

"Sure I know," Mason said. "He's Clint Adams, legend of the West."

"Then you know you can't—"

"Did you tell him?"

She fell silent.

"You didn't, did you?" he asked. "You lied to him, didn't you?"

She still didn't reply.

"How do you think he'd feel if he knew you'd been lying to him?" he asked. "How do you think he'd react?"

She stared at him and then said, "You can't come in."

"I don't want to come in," he said. "I just wanted to let you know I was here, that's all. I'm here and I'm not going away. I want my share, Jodi."

"You don't have a share," she said. "You don't deserve a share—"

"Yes, I do!" he snapped, cutting her off. "You know I do. I deserve a share, and I'm going to get it."

"You don't want a share," she said accusingly. "You want the whole thing."

"Come on, Jodi," Mason said, "why would I want the whole thing?"

"Because you're greedy."

"Me?" he asked innocently. "I'm not the greedy one, Jodi. I'm not the one who ran out—"

"I didn't run out."

"You ran out on me."

"We're divorced," she said. "I don't have to tell you where I go."

"You didn't have to tell me," he said. "I knew. I

know every move you're going to make before you
make it, kitten."

"Don't call me that."

"I called you that for nine years."

"Nine long years," she said, "and now they're over,
and I don't owe you anything."

She started to close the door, but he put his hand
out and stopped it.

"I'll be around, Jodi," he said. "I'll be around."

"I'll tell Clint."

"Go ahead," he said. "But if you tell him part of it
you'll have to tell him all of it, and how do you think
he'll react?"

"He'll . . . he'll kill you."

"I don't think so," he said, taking his hand away
from the door. "Somehow, I don't think so."

With that he walked away, leaving her there holding the door open. Before he reached the stairway,
though, he heard her slam it closed. He went down
with a satisfied smile on his face.

Jodi rushed to the window and saw her ex-
husband leave the hotel, cross the street, and enter
the other hotel. There was another man with him,
but she knew he'd have more than one. He was too
much of a coward not to surround himself with other
men.

He was there to watch, and to wait. Of that she
was sure. He wouldn't do anything until she found
what she was looking for. By then, maybe she'd be
able to come up with a story that would satisfy Clint.

Maybe.

THIRTY-SIX

"That's Woodsen," Katie said.

Woodsen might have been the same age as Key, but he looked as old as Jesse Williams—or maybe it was because he'd been exerting himself upstairs. He looked tired as he reached the bottom of the stairway.

"Ed, this feller's lookin' for you," Katie said.

Woodsen froze.

"What for?"

"Your friend Key brought him over," she said, "and it wasn't for any of my girls." Katie looked at Clint and said, "You don't know what you're missin'."

Clint looked at the girls and said, "I bet I do."

"Well then," she said, "come back when you have more time."

"Maybe I'll do that, ma'am."

Katie smiled and said, "It's madame."

Clint and Ed Woodsen left the whorehouse together.

"I need a drink," Woodsen said, "and then some sleep."

"How about if I buy you the drink?"

"What for?"

"Just for some conversation."

"About what?"

"About something that happened twenty years ago," Clint said. "Do you have a good memory?"

"That depends," Ed Woodsen said, "on how many drinks you're buyin'."

Minutes later they were in the saloon, lucky enough to find a table. Clint was uncomfortable because his back wasn't to a wall, but he decided that he wouldn't be there long enough for it to matter.

He hoped.

They each had a beer in front of them, and Woodsen looked happy.

"What do you want to talk to me about?" he asked.

"A wagon train."

"Which one?" Woodsen said. "I traveled with a lot of them over the years."

"This would have been one that left here in 1862, after the thaw."

"That's a long time ago," Woodsen said. "What do you want to know about it?"

"I'm looking for a man who might have been on it."

"What's his name?"

"Benton, Henry Benton."

Woodsen thought a moment.

"Does that name sound familiar to you?"

"No," Woodsen said after another moment, "it don't. Did you talk to Jimmy about this?"

"I did," Clint said.

"Because he could get you a look at the records, you know," Woodsen said. "They kept lists of the people who paid and traveled on those trains."

"I know," Clint said. "I've already seen the records and my man's name is not on it."

"Then whataya need me for?"

"He might have been traveling under another name."

"Why?" Woodsen asked. "Was he wanted by the law?"

"As a matter of fact, he was," Clint said. "Did you know anyone like that?"

Woodsen shook his head.

"If any of those men were wanted they sure didn't talk about it."

That made sense. Why would a wanted man announce it to anyone?

"Well, maybe you can tell me something about the wagon train routes," Clint said. "See, what I've heard is that my man died along the way. I have his daughter with me, and she'd like to find his grave."

"I'd like to help the little lady," Woodsen said. "Whataya want ta know?"

"Well, he was headed for Denver. Could you tell me what route the wagon train would have taken?"

"I use to know all the routes back then," Woodsen said, scratching his head.

"Can you remember now?"

"I guess I'd need to look at a map."

"Where could we find a map?"

"Well, over at the freight office, but they'd be closed now."

"Could we go over there tomorrow and have a look?"

"Sure thing," Woodsen said. "Uh, if I do this for you, though . . ."

"I'm willing to pay."

"Good, good," Woodsen said. "I won't ask for much, either. Just enough to go and see Lola again. She'll be wantin' to see me again after tonight, ya know?"

"Sure," Clint said, "I know. I only hope I'm in the same shape you are when I'm your age."

That puffed Woodsen's chest out a bit. Before leaving the saloon Clint got another beer and left it on the table in front of the man.

THIRTY-SEVEN

Mason was back in his room with the other man, looking out the window. He saw Clint go back to the hotel.

"So what did you accomplish?" the man asked.

"Just what I wanted to," Mason said. "I let her know I was here. I let her know that she can't get away from me that easily."

"It strikes me," the man said, "that you have something of an ego."

Mason looked at him.

"What's your point?"

"My point is, that makes me think you're going to want to go after Clint Adams."

He waited, and when there was no reply he went on.

"For that reason I think you better keep your other two . . . men on until this is over."

"Can't you handle Adams?"

"Not face-to-face," the man said. "That's not my game."

"You going to shoot him in the back?"

"No," the man said, "I don't do things that way, either. We just might have to outnumber him."

"Should I get even more men?"

"No," the man said, "you've got enough. It'll be hard enough to follow them as it is, without tipping Adams off—although why the woman—"

"My wife."

"—why your ex-wife wouldn't tell him about you—"

"I told you why," Mason said. "She knows better."

"Well, I guess we'll see about that, won't we?"

When Clint got back to the room, Jodi was still pouring over the list of names.

"Anything?"

She looked up as he entered.

"No," she said, "nothing yet."

"That's optimistic."

"We've got to find something," she said. "What did you find out?"

"I found a man who used to know all the routes the wagon trains would take."

"Used to? He doesn't anymore?"

"We're going to find that out tomorrow," Clint said.

"What happens tomorrow?"

"He and I are going over to the freight office to look at a map."

"I'm going to come with you."

"Fine," Clint said. "If he sees you, he might be even more eager to help."

"Because he's a man," she said knowingly.

"He's seventy-four years old and he still visits the whorehouse in town," Clint said. "All of these men—Jesse, Jimmy Key, and Ed Woodsen—are real characters. I like them."

"Well, hopefully between them your new friends can help us find my father."

"His grave."

"Yes."

"You do that a lot."

"What?"

"You say your father, not your father's grave. Why is that?"

"I don't know."

"Do you think he could still be alive?"

"I don't know."

"Would you want to find him alive?"

She shrugged.

"He left us," she said. "What would I say to him if he's alive?"

"What will you do if we find his grave?"

"I don't know!" she snapped. "Why are you pressing me like this?"

"Maybe there's something you're not telling me," Clint said.

She didn't answer.

"*Is* there something you're not telling me, Jodi?" he asked again.

She took a moment and then said, "No, Clint, there's nothing that I'm holding back from you."

"All right, then," he said. "It's getting late. Do you want to go and get something to eat?"

"Yes," she said. "I'm starved."

"Let's go, then."

"What about this?" she asked, pointing to the papers on the bed.

"We'll get them back together and return them tomorrow," Clint said. "Even if we can't find your father on these lists, maybe we'll find him if we can pinpoint the route the wagon train took."

"You'd still go looking?" she asked. "Even if his name is not on the list?"

"Like you said," Clint replied, "maybe he got on some other way. Come on, let's eat."

Mason watched Clint and Jodi leave the hotel.

"You going to watch them all night?" the other man in the room asked.

"Maybe."

"Are you still in love with your ex-wife?"

Mason didn't answer.

"I don't think they'll be going anywhere until at least tomorrow."

Mason turned and looked at the other man, then reached for his hat.

"Where are you going?"

"I want something to eat."

"I'll come with you—" the other man said, starting up from the bed.

"No," Mason said, "I want to eat alone."

The man leaned back on the bed.

"Don't do anything rash, Mason."

"I never do," Mason said, and left the room.

THIRTY-EIGHT

Over dinner Clint studied Jodi. She was quiet—so quiet that he was sure that something had happened. She had undergone some sort of change, but if he tried to talk to her about it she became tense and angry. He decided to leave it alone for a while.

"Why are you staring at me?" she demanded.

"I'm not—".

"Yes, you are."

"I'm looking at you," he said, "I'm not staring."

She put her fork down abruptly and looked at him.

"I'm sorry," she said. "The truth is I—I'm a bit confused, and I shouldn't be taking it out on you."

"Confused about what?"

"About why I'm looking for my father—for his

grave," she corrected herself. "It's just something I felt I had to do . . ."

"Are you having second thoughts?"

"It would be a little too late for that, wouldn't it?" she asked. "I mean, after coming all this way, that would be silly."

"No," Clint said, "having doubts wouldn't be silly—canceling the whole thing, *that* would be silly."

"No, I'm not going to cancel," she said. "I'm going to see this through to the end."

"Good for you."

"And I'll try not to bite your head off the rest of the way."

"That would be nice."

"In fact," she said, "when we get back to the room, maybe I'll just use my mouth to soothe your hurt feelings."

"My feelings aren't hurt."

"Is anything hurt?"

"Um, maybe I can find something . . ." he said, thinking about her mouth.

Roger Mason was standing outside the café where Clint Adams and Jodi were having dinner. He thought about the question he'd been asked a little while ago, whether or not he still loved his ex-wife.

Jodi was as beautiful as ever—*more* beautiful, even, than the day he'd met her, and the day they got married. She was obviously one of those women who improved with age. What would she look like, he wondered, ten years from now? He would like to be in a position to find out the answer to that question.

He wondered if, once they found what they were looking for, he'd be able to get her back.

He wondered if she was sleeping with Clint Adams.

He wondered how she'd react after they killed Clint Adams.

THIRTY-NINE

"Right there," Ed Woodsen said. "See that line? That's the route the wagon train would have taken."

He was pointing to a map on the wall of the freight office. Off to one side, fuming, was Steve Anderson, who had protested when Clint and Jodi Benton walked in with Woodsen just as he had the day before with Jimmy Key. Also, Woodsen treated the man the same way Key had, as an annoyance.

"Let me guess," Clint said to Woodsen as they approached the map. "You own part of this business?"

"A small part," Woodsen said. "Stevie's dad decided to leave me and Jimmy each a small piece—just enough to piss the kid off."

Now Jodi asked, "Are you sure, Mr. Woodsen?"

"Little lady," Woodsen said, "I'm sure that if this

wagon train was going to Denver, and then California, this is the route they would have taken. I can't say that your daddy was on it, though."

"I realize that."

Clint turned and looked at her.

"We're going to have to ride that route and look for grave markers."

"What if it's an unmarked grave?" she asked.

"We'll have to look for those, too."

She shook her head.

"This is silly," she said. "We *came* from Denver."

"Yes, we did," Clint said, pointing to the map, "but we didn't take that route. Even if we had, we wouldn't have known it. This is the only way we're going to be able to do this, Jodi."

"And what if we make that whole trip and we don't find it?" she asked.

"Well, we could always make it again."

"And again and again? I couldn't ask you to do that, Clint."

"Well, let's take it one step at a time," Clint said. "We'll have to outfit for this trip, with a packhorse and enough supplies."

"This is an old map," Woodsen said. "I don't even know why the kid leaves it up—unless he's sentimental, or somethin', but I don't think *that's* the reason."

"What's your point?" Jodi asked.

"Just that there will be some towns along the way that weren't there twenty years ago, miss. I don't think you'll need a packhorse. It would slow you down. I think you could restock your supplies along the way."

"Of course, you're right," Clint said, feeling dumb

for not noticing that the map was that old.

"When can we leave, then?" Jodi asked. "Today?"

"It's still early," Clint said, as it wasn't yet ten A.M. "I don't see why we can't pick up some supplies, saddle up, and get moving."

"Yes!" she said, clapping her hands together. "Mr. Woodsen, I can't thank you enough." Impulsively, she put her hands on the old man's shoulders and kissed his cheek.

"How much are you going to need—" Clint started to ask Woodsen as Jodi went rushing out the door.

"Forget it," Woodsen said, touching his cheek where she had kissed him. "You just find that little gal's daddy for her, and we'll be even."

"That's decent of you, Woodsen."

"Yeah," Woodsen said, "sure. You better get outta here before I change my mind."

Clint waved a hand and went out the door.

"Are you finished with my map?" Steve Anderson demanded peevishly.

Woodsen looked at him. The boy needed a trip to the woodshed. He always had, but his pa was too easy on him.

"Stevie," the old man shouted, "we been finished with this map for years. Take it down, for Chrissake!"

FORTY

Clint caught up to Jodi at the hotel, where they packed their gear and checked out of their room.

"We'll saddle the horses," Clint said as they left the hotel, "and then stop at the general store on the way out."

"Fine," she said excitedly, "the sooner we get started the better. Oh."

"What?"

"Do we need a copy of that map?"

"No," Clint said, "I remember the route. It's pretty straightforward once you know where to start from."

"I knew I needed you for some reason," Jodi teased.

•   •   •

As they were leaving the hotel, carrying their gear, they were watched from across the street. Pelter and Sullivan were watching from just inside the lobby. Roger Mason and the other man were watching from the window.

"There they go," the man said.

"Let's go after them."

"Not yet."

"But we have to follow them," Mason said.

"No, we don't," the man said. "We can track them. That way there's no danger of them seeing us."

"We might lose them."

"We won't be that far back," the man said. "If the trail starts to fade we can catch up and then follow them."

"Are you sure—"

"This is part of what you hired me to do, Mason," the man said. "Relax and let me do my job."

Mason nodded, then looked alarmed and started for the door.

"Where are you going?"

"I'd better go down and talk to those two morons before they do something stupid."

Clint and Jodi went to the livery to saddle their horses. Jimmy Key was there, sitting on his hay bale.

"Did you get what you wanted from Woodsen?" Key asked.

"Got enough to have a place to start," Clint said. "Thanks for your help, Jimmy."

"This the little lady you're tryin' to help?"

"It is."

"I'm Jodi Benton," she said, putting out her hand.

"I'd also like to thank you for your help."

Key shook her hand and said to Clint, "I can see why you want to help her so bad."

"Thank you," Jodi said.

They saddled their horses and rode out of the livery.

"Be back?" Key yelled.

"Not if we find what we want," Jodi called back.

They started riding over to the general store.

"What if we find your father's grave not far from here?" he asked. "This would be the closest town. We'd have to come back here."

"You're right," she said. "I wasn't thinking."

At the general store they went inside and Clint bought just enough supplies—coffee, bacon, jerky and such—to split into two separate sacks they could both carry.

Jodi waited outside while he went in to stock up. When he came back he saw her sitting in the saddle, swiveling about as if she was looking for someone.

"Is there something wrong?"

"Huh? Oh, no, nothing." She took the bag of supplies he handed her and tied it to her saddle. "You're used to traveling light, aren't you?"

"When I'm riding, yes," he said. He went on to explain that he had a gunsmithing rig and team he sometimes traveled with. Having a wagon made it easier to carry extra supplies.

"Where is your wagon now?"

"In Labyrinth, Texas, with a friend of mine. Sometimes I travel with it, sometimes without it. I didn't need it for the trip to Denver."

"So you're also a real gunsmith?"

"Yes."

"I thought it was—you know, just a name."

"As a name," he said, "it is just a name, if you know what I mean."

"I think I do," she said.

"All right," the man said to Mason. "Let's go and get our horses. We've given them enough of a head start."

He and Mason went downstairs and collected Pelter and Sullivan from the lobby. They walked to the livery and saddled their horses while the old liveryman watched them from a seated position on a bale of hay.

"Looks like a lot of people are headed out today," Jimmy Key said.

No one answered him.

"Where y'all headed?"

Still no answer. The only time one of them spoke to him was to settle their bill.

He watched as the four men rode out and knew instinctively that they were bad news—most likely for Clint and the girl.

If he was a few years younger, he might have followed them, but he hadn't been on a horse in five years, and even the thought of it made his butt hurt. He had problems with his butt. That was why he spent most of the day sitting on a bale of hay.

He went back to his hay and shook his head. They were just going to have to handle their own trouble without his help.

FORTY-ONE

In the old days, wagon trains often traveled the same path over and over again, so that eventually they actually did wear a path in the land that marked their route. That was years ago, though, and now there was no such path. Either the grass had grown high over it, or the land had grown hard. Clint and Jodi simply had to ride toward Denver, keeping their eyes open for anything that looked like an old grave.

"What if it's all grown over?" she asked. "Or so hard that we can't see it?"

"The land doesn't usually grow that hard over a grave site, Jodi. Sometimes grass does grow on them, but usually when people think enough of someone to bury them, they'll also provide a grave marker."

He didn't tell her that sometimes those grave

markers were shovel or pick handles, or pieces of wood pulled off a wagon. After twenty years those markers would be long gone. If, however, the grave was marked with stones, or a more permanent marker, they shouldn't have much trouble spotting it.

They rode steadily until an hour before sunset and then Clint suggested they stop for the night. They hadn't put much distance between themselves and the town because every so often one of them would spot something and they'd go off to investigate. At one point they actually did find a grave site and Jodi got very excited about it.

"Forget it, Jodi."

"We've got to dig it up."

He put his hand on her arm so she'd turned and looked at him.

"Look at the length of it."

The grave had been piled high with stones, and while some of the stones had fallen away over the years, there were still enough there to make out the size and shape of the grave.

"It's small," she said.

He nodded.

"It's a child's grave."

She lowered her head and shook it.

"Poor child," she said. "Poor mother."

"Come on," he said, "let's keep going."

Now he was gathering wood for a fire, and once the fire was started he let her cook while he took care of the horses.

When he returned to the fire she was staring back the way they had come. When she realized he was there she handed him a cup of coffee.

"Thanks."

He sat across the fire from her. During the ride from Denver he had taught her never to look into the camp fire, especially when it was dark. It ruined your night vision, and in the time it took for your eyes to adjust again someone—or something—could be on you.

"What's going on, Jodi?" he asked.

"What—what do you mean?"

"I mean what the hell is going on?" he asked, more forcefully this time.

"I don't know wha—"

"Sure you do. You've been different since last night. Did something happen?"

"Like what?" she asked, averting her eyes.

"And what about today?" he went on. "You keep acting like someone's watching you, or following you. Is that it? Is someone following us?"

"You would know that better than I would," she said. "Is someone following us?"

"Not that I can see," he said, "but you sure look like you're expecting someone."

"I'm not," she said, "I'm not expecting anyone."

"Well, maybe expecting is the wrong word," he said. "How about afraid? You're afraid that someone is going to come."

"I'm not . . . afraid."

"Well, there's something going on, and there's something you're not telling me."

"Like what?"

"I don't know," he said. "Maybe like the real reason you left Philadelphia?"

"To find my father's grave."

"No other reason?"

She hesitated, opened her mouth as if to speak, then paused again.

"To . . ." she started, but trailed off.

"Yes?"

She looked at him and said, "To get away from my ex-husband."

"Why?"

"Because I'm afraid of him," she said. "He . . . used to beat me, and when I divorced him he said he would never let me go."

"Do you think he can find you out here?"

She looked away.

"Jodi?"

"He already has," she said, without looking at him.

"What?"

"He was in town, last night," she said. "He was—he came to the room."

"When?"

"When you were out, just before we went to eat."

"What did he want?"

"He wanted me to know he was there," she said, looking at Clint now. "He wanted me to know that I couldn't get away from him that easy."

"Why didn't you tell me?"

"What would you have done?"

"I would have . . . talked to him."

"Just talked?" she asked.

"Well . . ."

"See, that's why I didn't want to tell you," she said. "It's bad enough I've got you traipsing all over the countryside looking for a grave. I didn't want you to think you had to . . . to defend me, as well."

"But if you're frightened of him—"

"One of you would have ended up dead, Clint," she

said hurriedly. "He's not alone, he brought some men with him."

"And you think they might be following us?"

"I thought they might."

"Well, no one is, or I would know," he said, "but they could be tracking us."

"Roger couldn't track us," she said. "He doesn't know anything about it."

"What about the men with him?"

"He probably brought them from Philadelphia," she said. "They're all from the city . . ."

"Is he smart?"

"What?"

"Roger," Clint said. "Is he smart?"

"He's very smart."

"Then he'd know enough to hire someone who could track," Clint said. "Otherwise how did they find you here?"

Jodi looked at him.

"You're right, Clint. What do we do?"

"Well, I could ride back and see if I can find them."

"They'd kill you."

"They wouldn't know I was there. I just want to see how many of them there are."

"And what about me?"

"You stay here and wait."

"But . . . what if they come here?"

"I don't think they will," Clint said.

"Why not?"

"Why didn't he do anything in town?"

"Because he's playing with me."

"Well, men like that don't usually finish playing this quickly," he said. "I don't think anyone will come, but if they do you have your gun."

"Yes."

"Could you do that?" he asked. "Could you shoot your ex-husband?"

"If he . . . threatened me, yes."

"All right, then." He dumped the remnants of his coffee in the fire and stood up. "I'll go on foot."

"You're going to walk?"

"They're probably not camped far away."

"What if . . . what if they're watching us now?"

"I don't think they are," he said. "I'd know, and if I didn't, Duke would."

"Your horse?"

Clint nodded.

"He can usually sense it when someone—or something—is watching us. You listen to him, Jodi. He'll let you know if someone other than me is approaching the camp."

"It's getting dark."

"I know," he said. "I'll wait until it is dark, and then I'll just go and see how many men we're dealing with."

FORTY-TWO

It was dark by the time Clint reached the camp. It wasn't hard to find. They had lit a fire, and since they were downwind of his camp they had prepared coffee and bacon. The smell of the cooking had not reached Clint's camp, but as he got closer it reached his nostrils.

He saw four men sitting around the fire. Two of them were talking, and the other two were silently consuming their meal.

One of the men who was talking had his back to him. Clint could see the other three, and did not know them.

Before he'd left camp he got a description of Roger Mason from Jodi, and it was easy to see that Mason was one of the two conversing men who was facing him.

While he watched, the two silent men finished eating, stood up, walked around some, and then found another place to sit, this time away from the fire and away from each other. They wore guns, but they did not wear them comfortably.

He watched, waiting to catch a look at the fourth man, but he finally had to give up. He wanted to get back to camp before Jodi started imagining that something had happened.

"Jodi, it's me," he called from just outside the circle of their campfire.

"Clint?"

He saw that she had her gun in her hands, held tightly in a two-handed death grip.

"Don't shoot, do you hear me? It's Clint."

"A-all right."

She lowered the gun and he walked into camp. She holstered the weapon and ran to him.

"It seemed like you were gone for hours."

He held her and said, "Everything's okay."

"Did you find them?"

"Yes."

"How many are there?"

"There's four of them," Clint said, "and I think I was right."

He explained how two of the men wore their guns awkwardly, and about the fourth man, whose face he couldn't see.

"You better have something to eat," she said. "I tried to keep the bacon from crisping, but—"

"I like crisp bacon," he said.

They sat around the fire and ate.

"What are we going to do now?" she asked.

"Well, we'll have to lose them, or face them," Clint said.

"Face them? Just the two of us?"

"You forget we're not in the city, Jodi," he said. "This is my territory, not theirs. Is Mason good with a gun?"

"Not that I know of."

"That means that three of them can't use one," Clint said.

"What about the fourth man?"

"Well, that's the problem," Clint said. "I really wouldn't want to try something until I know something about him."

"How do we find out?"

"Well, the first step is to get a look at him."

"How do we do that?"

"We'll have to turn the tables on them."

"How?"

He rubbed his jaw and said, "I'll have to think about that overnight. Meanwhile, why don't you get some sleep."

"What about you?"

"I'm going to stand watch."

"You said they wouldn't come into our camp tonight."

"I said I didn't think they would," Clint said. "I'll stand watch just to be on the safe side."

"You can't stand watch all night. You'll fall asleep in the saddle. We'll take turns."

"You wouldn't know what to look for."

"You can tell me," she said, "and I'll rely on Duke, too."

"Jodi, you can't—"

"No, *you* can't . . . you can't stay up all night. I'll take the first watch. When should I wake you?"

"Look—"

"Let's not argue, Clint," she said. "When?"

"Oh, all right," he said. "Wake me in four hours."

"Is that enough?"

"It's plenty of sleep, believe me. Besides, I might want to take another walk, maybe at first light."

"To try to see the other man?"

"Yes."

"All right, then," she said. "Tell me what to do, and then get some sleep."

"Don't you think one of us should go and watch their camp?" Mason asked.

"No," the man said. "They have to sleep, don't they?"

"What if they just keep going?"

"They won't. They don't know we're here, Mason. They have to rest and so do their horses. They won't leave until first light."

"What if we oversleep?"

The man laughed, remembering their ride from Denver to Council Bluffs. The first night Mason and the other two men slept on the ground they didn't get much sleep. After that they slept, but fitfully, and always complained the next day about the aches and pains.

"We won't," he said. "We won't."

FORTY-THREE

Clint decided overnight that they had two options. First, he could sneak back to their camp and try to get a look at that fourth man. Second, they could get up before first light and continue on. Depending on how good a tracker the fourth man was, they might lose them.

He thought it over for a few hours and decided to try the second option. The first was too risky. He'd have to go back before first light so he could be there when they got up, and there was still no guarantee that he'd get to see the man's face—and if he did see him, he might not know him. This way they'd put some distance between themselves and the four men even before they woke up.

It was two hours before first light when he shook Jodi awake.

Mason, Pelter, and Sullivan woke at first light. The fourth man had already made a pot of coffee, and each man had a cup.

"What about breakfast?" Sullivan asked sourly. Of the three city men he was the one who hated sleeping on the ground the most.

"We'll have to do without," the fourth man said.

"Why?"

"Well, basically because I say so," he replied, "but I want to get started as soon as he does so they don't get too much of a head start."

"You afraid you're gonna lose 'em?" Pelter asked.

The man didn't answer.

"That's enough," Mason said to the two men. "Get the horses saddled."

"I'll saddle my own," the man said.

"Wasn't gonna do it, anyway," Pelter mumbled.

As they walked off, the man said to Mason, "I don't admire your taste in employees, other than myself."

"Don't let them fool you," Mason said. "In Philadelphia they're good men to have."

"We ain't in Philadelphia," the other man said, "are we?"

A short time later they were sitting astride their horses, looking down at Clint and Jodi's former campsite. Pelter and Sullivan were looking very satisfied with themselves.

"What happened?" Mason asked.

"I'll tell you in a minute," the other man said, dismounting.

He put his hand over the campfire ashes.

"They didn't leave that long ago," he said, touching the ashes now. "Maybe a couple of hours."

"You said they wouldn't do that," Mason said.

"I know what I said."

He walked around the camp, studying the ground. He had walked to the far end of the camp when Pelter looked at Mason and asked, "What the hell is he doin'?"

"I don't know," Mason said, hoping he hadn't made a mistake after all in hiring the man.

When he came back he looked up at the three of them.

"He knows we're here."

"How could he know that?" Mason asked.

"She probably told him," the man said. "You said she wouldn't."

"How do you know he knows?" Sullivan asked.

"He scouted our camp last night."

"What?" Mason snapped.

"He went back on foot and found our camp," the man said. "He knows there are four of us on his trail, that's why he left early. He's trying to lose us."

"But he isn't going to, is he?" Mason asked.

"No," the man said, mounting up again, "he isn't."

FORTY-FOUR

"Do you think we lost them?" Jodi asked, following the question with a yawn.

"Who knows?" Clint said. "I guess that will depend on how good that fourth man is."

"Clint?"

"What?"

She hesitated, then said, "Never mind."

Something was on her mind, and she was going to have to get to it in her own time. There was something more than a possessive ex-husband happening here.

They rode for half a day, with Clint watching their back trail. He became convinced that the four men would catch them easily. Every time Jodi saw something she thought might be a grave she rode off to investigate it. It wasted so much time that the four men *had* to catch them.

"Do you want to stop for lunch?" he asked her.

"No," she said, "I want to keep going."

He took out a piece of beef jerky and passed it to her, then took one for himself. That was the extent of their lunch.

"What is it?" she asked.

"There's something over there," he said, pointing.

It was about three P.M. when he saw it.

"I see it," she said. "Jesus, it's a cross."

It was indeed a proper grave marking in the shape of a cross.

They both rode for it, Clint reaching it before she did.

He dismounted and walked to it. The cross was blank except for the initials: H. B.

Henry Benton.

This had to be it.

He heard her coming up behind him on foot. When she saw the initials she caught her breath.

"This is it."

"It looks like it," Clint said. "You know, in our haste to leave I forgot to get a small spade. I didn't even think of something to wrap the remains in. Of course, we could go to the nearest town and get the undertaker—"

"Clint," she said, grabbing his arm, "we have to get away from here."

"Why?"

She pulled on his arm.

"Come on, before they get here."

"Why, Jodi?"

"I don't want Roger to know that we found it," she said, pulling on him desperately. He wouldn't let her budge him.

"I'm not moving," he said, "not until I get some explanations, Jodi."

She stopped pulling on him and looked around them. There was no one in sight.

"Clint, I can explain later—"

"Explain now," he said. "What's buried here besides your father—if Henry Benton is your father."

"He is!" she snapped. "That is, he was, before he left us."

"How could you be interested in a man who left you all that time ago?" he asked. "There's got to be something else."

"What?"

Nervously, she looked around.

"The quicker you tell me, the quicker we can get going."

"All right," she said, closing her eyes for a moment, then opening them, "all right . . . there's money down there."

"Money?"

She nodded.

"How much?"

"I don't know," she said. "Maybe as much as fifty thousand dollars."

"Fifty—where did it come from? How do you know it's there?"

"Clint, we have to go! I'll tell you later. We have to leave before they—"

"Too late," Clint said, looking past her.

She turned and saw the four riders standing at the top of a low hill.

"No," she said.

"Finish your story," he said.

"But . . . they're here."

"They're not going to try anything," Clint said, "not yet. Finish your story."

"It's very simple," she said. "Last year I found my mother's diaries. She wrote everything down. I finally found out why my father left us."

"Why?"

"He and a partner of his stole some money."

"From where?"

"I don't know."

"How much?"

"Maybe a hundred thousand dollars."

"Go on."

"He and his partner left Philadelphia to come west with the money, to escape the police. My father said he was going to Denver and he would send for my mother. He never did."

"And?"

"A year later my mother got a letter from my father's partner. His name was Christopher King. He said in his letter that my father had died on the wagon train from Council Bluffs to Denver. King said he buried my father, and the money, so that my mother could come and get it. She never did, and then she died."

"Why didn't she come?"

"She didn't want the money."

"But you found her diaries, and you wanted the money?"

"That's right," she said. "Why shouldn't I have it?"

"It's stolen."

"From who? I don't know. Who would I return it

to? No, I figured this money was coming to me,
Clint."

"And what were you going to do when we dug up
the grave and found it? Act surprised?"

"I don't know," she said, "I don't know how I
would have reacted, but I do know one thing."

"What?"

"I would have shared it with you."

"But not with your husband, huh?"

"Ex-husband."

"Does he know about the money?"

"Yes," she said bitterly. "I was foolish enough to
show him the diaries."

"So he wants the money, and not you."

"He wants both," she said, "but I don't want him
to have either."

"Well, he's here now," Clint said.

"What are they waiting for?" she asked, shielding
her eyes so she could see the four men.

"The right time, I guess."

"And when will that be?"

"Maybe," he said, "after we dig up the money—if
there's any money there."

"What?"

"You've got to remember, Jodi," Clint said, "if
what you're telling me is finally the truth—"

"It is."

"—you've got to remember that your father and
this feller King stole that money. They were thieves."

"So?"

"So why would a thief leave money in the ground?"
Clint asked her. She looked stunned. "After all, how
far from a thief is a liar?"

FORTY-FIVE

"Are we gonna wait for them to do something?" Sullivan asked.

"What are they doing?"

"They've found it," Mason said.

"Found what?" Pelter asked.

"See that cross?"

All four men squinted.

"It's a grave," Sullivan said. "Is that what this has been about? A grave?"

"Not just any grave," Mason said. "Jodi's father's grave."

"I didn't know she had a father," Pelter said.

"Everybody has a father, Dennis," Sullivan said.

Mason looked at the fourth man.

"What do you think we should do?"

"Sit here awhile and see what they do," he said.

"What do we want them to do?" Sullivan asked.

Mason had a decision to make now. Sullivan and Pelter knew nothing about the money that was supposed to be in that grave.

"I think we should go and talk to them," he said finally.

"Well, let's do something."

"Dennis, you and Sullivan stay here."

"What?"

"Just do it." Mason looked at the fourth man and said, "Come on."

"They're coming," Jodi said suddenly.

"Two of them are."

"Is that the other man?"

"That's him."

"Do you know him?"

"I can't see his face yet, but he looks—no, it couldn't be."

"Couldn't be who?"

"Is it?"

Clint waited until the two men had come closer before shaking his head and saying, "It is."

"It is who?"

He didn't answer, and then the two men reached them and did not dismount.

"Hello, Jodi."

"Go away, Roger."

"Is that any way to talk to your husband?"

"Ex-husband."

"How did you get involved in this, Brett?" Clint asked.

Brett Garner looked at Clint and smiled.

"I can't quite make enough gambling to maintain my life-style, Clint."

"So you take odd jobs?"

"Sometimes."

"What's your job here?"

"My job was to find you and the lady."

"Where did they pick you up?" Clint asked.

"Same place she got you," Garner said. "Denver."

"Do you know what it's about?"

"Sounds like a marital problem to me."

"To me, too," Clint said, "but it's also about fifty thousand dollars that's supposed to be buried here."

"I didn't know anything about that."

"You told him?" Mason demanded, glaring at Jodi.

"Yes."

"Kill him," Mason said to Garner.

The gambler gave Mason a slow look.

"Kill him yourself, Mason."

"I'm no match for him," Mason said.

"Well, neither am I."

"I'm paying you well."

"I won't be able to spend it dead."

"What about your other two men, Mason?" Clint asked.

"They'll kill you—"

"Not with their guns, they won't. They're not even wearing them right. Tell me, do they know about the money?"

Mason didn't answer.

"I see they don't. I guess that's why you left them way over there."

"The money is mine!" Mason said.

"It belongs to me!" Jodi said. "It was my father's."

"He stole it."

"Stole it?" Garner asked. "I'm a little lost here."

"So what?" Jodi asked. "We don't know who he took it from, so we can't return it."

"You could return it to the law and let them decide what to do with it."

"Wait a minute," Garner said. "What's all that money doing in the ground?"

"Miss Benton believes that her father's partner— the man with whom he stole the money—buried it here with her father when he died."

Garner looked incredulous.

"Why would he do that?"

"It was my father's money."

Garner looked at Clint.

"Is she serious?"

"I'm afraid she is."

"What are you talking about?" Mason demanded.

"Mr. Mason," Clint said, "you can dig to your heart's content but my guess is you're not going to find any money there."

"What?"

"All you'll find is a body."

"Which probably has a hole in it," Garner said.

"From what?" Jodi asked. "My father died of natural causes."

"Like a bullet in the back," Garner said.

"Or the head," Clint said.

"Are you saying that King killed my father?"

"And took his money?" Mason asked.

Garner and Clint exchanged a look, and then Clint said, "That's our guess."

"That's . . . not right," Mason said.

"Dig it up, then," Clint said.

"Clint—"

"You lied to me, Jodi," Clint said, "several times over. I'm done."

"But I need you."

"You've got Roger here," Clint said.

"But the money—"

"There's not going to be any money."

She looked at her ex-husband.

"Roger!"

Mason turned and waved his other two men on.

"We'll dig it up," he said to Jodi. "It has to be there."

The two riders came on the run with their guns in their hands.

Both Clint and Garner drew their guns and fired. Their bullets struck the ground in front of the two running horses. The animals reared, tossing their riders onto their asses. As the two men landed, they let go of their guns, which went flying.

"We don't want any trouble, Mason, do we?" Clint asked.

"No, no trouble," Mason said. "Let me get this straight, Adams. If there's money in there you don't want any part of it?"

"I'm betting there's no money there," Clint said.

"And if you lose," Mason said, "you lose."

"Right."

"And you?" Mason asked Garner.

"Since I didn't know anything about any money anyway," Garner said, "I'll bet it's not there, too."

"Fine," Mason said.

Sullivan and Pelter got to their feet and started looking for their guns.

"Never mind your guns," Mason said. "Get over here and start digging!"

"Clint—" Jodi said.

"Good-bye, Jodi," Clint said. He looked at Garner. "Which way are you headed?"

"Same way as you, for a while, anyway."

"Let's go, then."

They had ridden a short way when they heard what sounded like a woman's voice echo, "No-o-o-o!"

And then a man's voice cried, "Arg-h-h-h!"

They looked at each other.

"No money?" Garner asked.

Clint nodded and said, "No money."

Watch for

TRIPLE CROSS

176th novel in the exciting GUNSMITH series
from Jove

Coming in August!

If you enjoyed this book, subscribe now and get...

TWO FREE

A $7.00 VALUE—

If you would like to read more of the very best, most exciting, adventurous, action-packed Westerns being published today, you'll want to subscribe to True Value's Western Home Subscription Service.

Each month the editors of True Value will select the 6 very best Westerns from America's leading publishers for special readers like you. You'll be able to preview these new titles as soon as they are published, *FREE* for ten days with no obligation!

TWO FREE BOOKS

When you subscribe, we'll send you your first month's shipment of the newest and best 6 Westerns for you to preview. With your first shipment, two of these books will be yours as our introductory gift to you absolutely *FREE* (a $7.00 value), regardless of what you decide to do. If you like them, as much as we think you will, keep all six books but pay for just 4 at the low subscriber rate of just $2.75 each. If you decide to return them, keep 2 of the titles as our gift. No obligation.

Special Subscriber Savings

When you become a True Value subscriber you'll save money several ways. First, all regular monthly selections will be billed at the low subscriber price of just $2.75 each. That's at least a savings of $4.50 each month below the publishers price. Second, there is never any shipping, handling or other hidden charges—*Free home delivery*. What's more there is no minimum number of books you must buy, you may return any selection for full credit and you can cancel your subscription at any time. A TRUE VALUE!

J. R. ROBERTS
THE
GUNSMITH